Sex, Love, & Food

Sex, Love, & Food

The intricacies of what's delicious

LATEEFAH WIELENGA

ISBN: 0692910867
ISBN 13: 9780692910863

Contents

Quail in Rose Petal Sauce

12 roses, preferably red
12 chestnuts
2 tsp. butter
2 tsp. cornstarch
2 drops attar of roses
2 Tbsp. anise
2 Tbsp. honey
2 cloves garlic
6 quail
1 pitaya

Brown the quail in butter and season with salt and pepper.

Remove the petals carefully from the roses. Ground the petals with anise in a mortar. Separately, brown the chestnuts in a pan, remove the peels and cook them in water. Then puree them. Mince the garlic and slightly brown in butter; when it is transparent, add it to the chestnut puree along with the honey, then ground pitaya and the rose petals, and salt to taste.

To thicken the sauce slightly, you may add two tablespoons of cornstarch.

Last, strain through a fine sieve and add no more than 2 drops of attar of roses. As soon as the seasonings have been added, remove sauce from heat. The quail should be immersed in the sauce for 10 minutes to infuse them with the flavor, and then removed.

Place the quail on a platter, pour the sauce over them and garnish with a single perfect rose in the center and rose petals scattered all around.

Source: **"Like Water for Chocolate," a novel by Laura Esquivel**

One

"You couldn't have picked a better day to go out on me." Colette says softly as she walks through the kitchen, carrying a big bucket – complete with ice cubes – into her backyard. She slowly walks over to the water faucet and places the bucket under the spigot. She turns on the water and watches it flow over the ice. Once the bucket is full, Colette reaches down and places a thirsty dish towel into the icy cold water. As she brings the soaked towel from the bucket, she lifts it above her head and wrings it free of liquid, as the water travels all over her head, face, neck, and down her arms. She dips the towel again and squeezes the dripping cloth over her chest. Once she's cooled off, Colette wraps the towel around her neck and whispers,

"I got you broken air conditioner," and smiles.

Refreshed, Colette walks back into the kitchen – which now seems bearable – and continues chopping vegetables.

The kitchen has high ceilings and lots of windows looking out onto the flower garden. There's a large taupe marble island in the center of the room, which is accommodating seasonings, spices, two thick, round wooden cutting boards, which stand on small ornate legs, and a knife block. On one side of the island are four, white leather, waffle-back bar stools. Three square, glass box-shaped chandeliers, each containing suspended lights, give the illusion of fireflies. The walls are painted the color of sand with white trim. The finest appliances grace this gourmet kitchen. The commercial range boasts eight gas burners and a double oven. The refrigerator is designed to resemble the sleek kitchen cabinets. With the exception of one large, transparent wall exposing myriad types of glasses, which looks like a piece of art, one would not be convinced this was the kitchen.

There's going to be a party here tonight. Jason's little sister, Janis, turned 30 years old today and she's completed the final draft of her first off-Broadway play. Tonight's a huge deal and Colette wants everything to go smoothly. The fact that she and Jason, her husband of three years, aren't getting along, isn't making this any easier. This is the couple's first serious misunderstanding. The tension between them has lasted for the past couple of days. It's been quite challenging. What was so different about this time? For some reason, neither Colette nor Jason has been willing to acquiesce. What used to be so simple to do, so natural for them both, has become an insurmountable chore. Such resistance. There was a time when there was no need for words, looks and touches would suffice. A lingering glance, lowering of the eyes, moving a bit closer, a finger touches the back of a hand …

How bittersweet, Colette thinks as she chuckles, thinking about her life – life before Jason – before she'd ever known love could be like this. Better than the anticipation of a fine meal with beautiful wine; more intoxicating than a warm night under a Harvest Moon. Colette remembers when she first met him. How everything seemed to be aligned and the universe set it all up. It all fell together so effortlessly.

She begins to remember the night she actually met Jason. It was a Thursday evening five years ago. Colette walked into Tin Roof restaurant in Manhattan Beach. She liked the ambiance and the energy of the people.

"This place feels good to me" she said to her best friends Lauren and Pamela.

"I'm glad we made this decision."

As they walked into the restaurant there was a bar to the left, many people were seated there for the wine tasting event. Tables had been rearranged to accommodate the customers. The restaurant has an outdoor patio area at the entrance and an outdoor seating area on the south side next to The Vintage Wine Shoppe, almost connected to it. When looking at Tin Roof, one can see its Spanish style with its red-tiled roof and bougainvillea. When Colette surveyed the room, she saw a lot of good looking guys. Bruno Mars' *Nothin' On You* was playing; the lyrics made her feel special. She gently moved her body to the rhythm of the music, noticing the smell of garlic and various spices that filled the room with comfort. The murmuring of the guests helped Colette feel all too pleased that she'd decided to attend this wine tasting. She released a happy sigh, looked at her girlfriends, and smiled.

When they ordered their wine flights, Colette glanced over the shoulder of their server and saw a really handsome gentleman. There was just something about him. It wasn't his height or his physique that impressed her. It was something she couldn't quite put her finger on. *What was it?* she found herself asking. Colette directed her attention to her girlfriends,

"When you get a chance – and don't be obvious – look at the tall guy standing at the fourth table. He's wearing a white-silk shirt, tan colored slacks and brown Armani loafers. Is there something about him or is it just me?"

Pamela casually glanced at the guy approvingly.

"He is nice," she said.

"But so are many of the guys in here. Look at him." Pamela said as she pointed out another nice-looking guy with sexy, piercing eyes.

"I agree, coming here tonight was a great idea," Lauren said.

"Leave it to me to get us out of our social rut. But I've got to say a second time that that guy is so ..." Colette said, and her voice trailed off.

She couldn't articulate her feelings about the guy across the room. His skin was smooth with a golden glow. He had a cleft chin and his brown eyes twinkled when he laughed. His body was strong. It was easy to tell just by the way his loose-fitting clothes draped over his sinewy body.

olette had spent the past few nights scanning the internet for places to go that were outside of her comfort zone. When she found a wine tasting happening in Manhattan Beach, she called Pamela and Lauren.

"Let's get out of town Thursday night and go to the South Bay. There's a wine tasting I think will be fun. Interested?"

Her girlfriends agreed they all needed a change from Huntington Beach.

"Great! Let's meet here on Thursday at about 6." Colette pushed the end button on her iPhone and let it drop to her king-sized bed. She walked into her closet and scanned her wardrobe. Her eyes passed her huge, floor mirror and her gaze went right to her soft, just past her shoulders, sandy brown, naturally curly hair. Her skin is a smooth, caramel brown, which match her big hazel eyes. Colette's lips are full and perfect. She stands about 5'8", and wears a size 6 dress. Her purple, oversized lightweight sweater hangs off her right shoulder, exposing a blue bra strap. Her Joe's jeans are soft from the consistent wear. She thought she might wear the Nanette Lepore dress she'd just gotten from Neiman's last week. *Hmm, Kate Spade shoes and hand bag or those cute Donald Pliner booties? I'll figure it out tomorrow,* she thought, as she stood in front of her mirror and critiqued her strikingly beautiful face, perfect figure and hazel eyes. Even though Colette is modest and would never admit to how stunning she is, she has learned to accept herself and her beauty.

She turned off the lights, closed the door to her closet and went into her office to finish the work she'd brought home with her. She's an account executive for a successful insurance brokerage firm. She felt like she was in heaven when she initially got the promotion. She could buy all of the clothes she wanted, eat out whenever she decided, and travel. But after a time she realized she was only in it for the salary. She had taken that job because she didn't want to be without money. The lack of money stressed her out, made her feel inadequate. When she was in elementary school, she had a best friend named Marilyn, whose mother gave her a big allowance. Colette wasn't able to purchase food from the local burger stand after school, but Marilyn could, so she would always pay for Colette. Because of that, Colette decided then she would always have enough money to not only provide for herself, but for others as well.

When Colette realized, she wasn't sure what she really wanted to do with her life, she was given a promotion. With that, and all the praise from her family and friends, Colette resolved she would be there for quite some time. She was now financially secure and on her way up the corporate ladder; wherever that led. *This place has never been a fit for me. I know why I accepted the position, but I never considered money would be the chain that wound bind me.*

Colette graduated top of her class – summa cum laude – from Vanguard University with an MBA in finance. She knew what that prestigious honor would do for her career – her life. But she found herself wondering, more often than not, if life didn't have more to offer.

Brushing off those thoughts, she began reviewing the documents that desperately needed her attention. Ever the procrastinator when disinterested, Colette had let the project linger far too long. It could have been completed a few days after having been assigned to her. Now she wishes it was finished and on her boss' desk. *If only I could cross my arms, blink my eyes and nod my head, I'd be rid of this!* Her lips curled into a little smile as she knew she was making too big a deal of it. It was almost the weekend and she's had plenty of time to get it done.

Colette began reviewing a file that her boss had emphasized as a priority. Before she realized, it was 1:30 in the morning. "Where does the time go?" Colette mumbled and began putting her work away. All caught up and even ahead of the game, she felt a pang of fear rush over her. It was times like this that brought the blanket of melancholy her way. No matter how Colette tried to escape her unhappiness with her career, it always made itself known. Fear that she would never know what she was really supposed to be doing with her life, uncertainty about her desires, not really aware of whom she is or where she is going. *Who am I and what am I supposed to be doing? What will satisfy me?* Colette cried out in the night.

She closed her laptop, arranged the papers in an organized pile and turned off her desk lamp. She stood up and stretched, arms over head, fingers extended, legs clinched: "Ahh" was the sound that the feeling released and Colette went into the bathroom to wash her face, brush her teeth and floss. She turned on the water and listened to it softly dance around the porcelain as she starred at herself in the mirror. No thoughts really, just that slight feeling of dread about going back to that office and doing that same unfulfilling work tomorrow. She looked at her eyes and noticed the sadness there. She then, mechanically reached for her cleansing cream and washed her face. Blotting it dry, Colette reached in the medicine cabinet and got the toothpaste and the floss. She reached over and got her electric toothbrush, applied the toothpaste and began brushing her teeth. Two minutes did the trick. Colette flossed, rinsed her mouth, wiped the sink and ironically went into the kitchen.

Opening the refrigerator door, Colette looked in and decided to get her gelato out of the freezer. Sea salt caramel; her favorite. She took it out, got a spoon and stood there in the kitchen and had two spoons full. Placing the spoon in her dishwasher, she went to bed. As she lay there in comfort, she went over a list of everything she had to be thankful for. Feeling fortunate, despite her career dissatisfaction, she closed her eyes and slept.

Colette is an old soul and a very creative person. She listens to her intuition and usually knows things that she was not told. Her desire has been to create; her passion – fashion and interior design. Colette's parents had lofty plans for her that did not include the arts. They wanted her to be in the corporate world. So, never receiving the encouragement needed to follow her dream, she found herself working for an insurance firm and accepting her current position.

Always waking up naturally, with her eyes closed, Colette began claiming her day. Once she told herself how her day was going to play out, she opened her eyes and silently thanked her comfortable bed and her soft, decadent sheets. She pulled the sheets from her body and left her bed with ease. She walked over to the big windows and pulled back the drapes. The sun was bright at this early hour. Colette then went to her winged-back chair in her room and began her meditation. Two times each day, for 20 minutes, Colette meditated. She's been that kind of girl since she can remember. Always looking for the answers to the mysteries of life, Colette's trajectory has been spiritual. Meditation is her constant, and she hardly ever misses a session, especially before going to the office.

That evening, when Colette pulled into her garage, she was excited. She'd left the office early to meet the girls at 6 o'clock. She walked into the house and into her bedroom, turned on the television to what she'd DVR'd a few days before – Amy Schumer. As Colette listened to Amy, she was laughing and preparing for the night. She'd decided to wear her Nanette Lepore dress, and her Kate Spade shoes, without the bag. She thought she'd just bring the purse she always carried. The one she had gotten in Italy last year. No name, just a nice leather bag. Colette hopped in and out of the shower. She dressed quickly and the doorbell rang like clockwork.

Opening the door with a big smile, Colette greeted her friends,

"Hello ladies, you look fabulous."

"So do you," Lauren said, and then added,

"I love your dress."

Pamela agreed with Lauren and the three began to walk toward the kitchen.

"Are you excited to begin our new journey away from our comfort zone?" Pamela asked.

"Nervous is more like it." Colette said.

"I'd like to have a glass of wine before we drive up. Who wants to join me?" She asked.

Lauren was quiet as Colette opened the glass cabinet and removed three large wine glasses, excellent for the cabernet. Pamela noticed Lauren was uncomfortable when Lauren pursed her lips and looked at the floor – that's what she does when she feels that way. Pamela then made a suggestion.

"We should call Uber (a private driving service, much like a taxi service) to avoid any problems driving after having wine tonight. We won't have to worry about anything."

"That's a great idea because it would be horrible if we got stopped for driving under the influence, or worse, if we were in an accident and someone was unnecessarily hurt." Colette stated.

"You can all stay here tonight if you like. Let's just be safe and have fun." Colette offered.

Lauren thought about Uber and leaving her car, when Pamela looked at her and said,

"Really Lauren? What sense would it make for you to drive home? We're going to take my car up anyway. I don't mind leaving it in Manhattan Beach."

Once Lauren heard that, she relaxed, and said,

"Be generous with your pour Colette, you know Caymus is one of my favorite reds."

The energy in the room lightened as Colette poured generously, and the ladies made a toast, to new beginnings. Silently, Colette thought, *Nervous – now I wonder what that's about.*

They took their wine glasses and went into the living room. Colette sat in her favorite eggshell white, quilted-chaise, while the others sat on the matching oversized couch, which was peppered with muted-colored pillows. Classical music was wafting through the house and the girls were talking about tonight.

"Do you mind changing the music to something more upbeat to help us get in the mood for this wine tasting?" Lauren said with humor.

Lauren and Danny had been broken up for more than six months now and she wasn't sure how she was feeling about possibly meeting someone new. *Yes, I've agreed to needing to get out of my relationship rut, but am I?*

"Oh,"

Colette sang.

"Somebody's perking up!"

Colette changed the music immediately to John Legend's *P.D.A. (We Just Don't Care)*, and the girls started dancing around the living room.

"Let's just leave our cars here and take Uber up *and* back," Colette said.

"Better yet, let's just call a driver!" Pamela said.

"Now you're talking," Colette said.

The girls agreed. They didn't call Uber, they called for a car. The car arrived and the friends took one last look in the mirror, the last sips of Caymus, and closed the door behind them.

Red Roses

Interrupting her thought of things coming together so effortlessly, Colette's ringing cellphone brings her out of her reverie and she reaches over to answer it. She knows by the melody of her phone that Jason is on the line.

"Hi sweetheart," she says, wishing things were better between them.

"Hey Baby, how's your day going?" Jason knows he's the one responsible for the tension – and doesn't know how to begin the conversation.

"I'm just calling to check in with you to see if you need anything. I'll be leaving the restaurant in about 30 minutes," Jason says.

"No, I'm good," Colette says.

"But the air conditioner went out a few hours ago," she says hesitantly.

"Did you call it in?" Jason asks.

"Yes, I did," Colette says.

"Great. I think we'll be all right by tonight," Jason assures her.

"Do you still think you'll be home in time to prepare the quail?" Colette asks.

"I certainly do," Jason says with a lilt.

"One more question. 'Did you get the red roses?'" Colette shyly asks.

"Of course, I got them. I love you Colette," Jason says.

There is a slight pause before she says,

"I love you too. See you soon."

Colette realizes she is behaving as if she and Jason have just met and this is a first date. She thinks, *Why am I so nervous? I can't believe Jason still has this effect on me. He still gives me butterflies. I'm always excited to see him, and I just can't stand it when we're fighting.*

Colette is deep in thought as she slowly walks over to the pantry and removes a bar of dark, Swiss chocolate. She pulls back the golden foil. *The rich remedy for chasing my blues away*, she thinks as she bites a piece of the chocolate and tastes its bitter-sweetness, while also experiencing its magic – no matter how temporary.

There have only been a few times since she and Jason have been married that this has happened. This feeling of distance between them. This feeling that there are things about him she doesn't know. She stands in the pantry for what seems to be a few minutes longer.

She walks out of the pantry and heads back to the kitchen island where many of her ingredients rest. She's feeling uncertain about Jason. *Did I say something last night that triggered this behavior? Or any other night for that matter?* Not really sure about what is going on between them, Colette begins busying herself with tiding up the kitchen. She wants to continue preparing the meal with some semblance of order. She decides to review the menu for the party, which is tonight. She has food ideas she believes their guests will enjoy eating, but she hasn't yet solidified anything. Of course, her favorite food store, The Gourmet Shop in Five Points, will have everything she'll need if she doesn't have it in her pantry or freezer. As Colette begins thinking about, and rearranges, her menu, she hears Jason come in the door. Thank goodness, he makes his own hours. They'll have plenty of time to pull this off.

"Colette," he calls, and the door closes behind him.

He quickly walks through the foyer carrying three dozen beautiful red roses. He continues down the hall and into the kitchen. When he sees Colette, Jason hesitates, places the flowers on the counter and walks slowly toward her. Hearing Jason come into the house surprises Colette. She didn't expect him so soon. Her heart begins to pound. She looks up, startled. "I didn't expect you so soon. I thought you were still at the restaurant," she says to the man she so deeply loves. Jason looks directly at his wife and slowly approaches her. When he reaches Colette, he places her face in his hands, leans toward her and kisses her passionately. Colette thinks his lips taste like fresh Georgia peaches drenched in brandy. Intoxicating. She returns the kiss. Feeling her legs weaken and her head spin, Colette begins removing Jason's shirt. Jason runs his hands through Colette's hair, pulling it ever so slightly, and begins undressing her. There are no words spoken. A look of love, a passionate kiss, a tugging of the hair and the removal of a shirt ...

Broiled Brussels Sprouts

10 medium Brussels sprouts (cut in half)
Basil olive oil
Salt
Pepper
Garlic cloves
1 red bell pepper (julienned)

Two

The car pulled into Manhattan Village from the Marine street entrance. They passed Ralphs grocery store, the Corner Bakery and Islands restaurant. Across the parking lot was Tin Roof. The driver turned left onto the parking area and drove directly in front of the restaurant and parked the car. The girls waited in the back until the driver walked around to the passenger side of the car and opened the door for them. Pamela took his hand and exited the back of the car. Next was Lauren, followed by Colette. People were sipping wine from flights on a front patio. When they walked into the Spanish-styled restaurant, Colette spotted three empty seats at the bar to her left. She pointed in that direction and they all headed that way. Seated, the three ordered wine flights from the cute server. Colette noticed something of interest over the shoulder of the server. …

As Colette was contemplating the nice-looking guy in linen, she caught *his* eye, and without hesitation he made his way across the room toward her. Colette looked over at Lauren and Pamela to alert them to what she believed was about to occur. They were ordering appetizers for the table, which included the Brussels sprouts Colette wanted to try, when the gentleman was

standing next to her. Smiling warmly, Colette looked up at him as he introduced himself.

"Hello," he began, and Colette thought, *I even love his voice, it's like silk.*

"I'm Jason English. I saw you when you came in and I couldn't live with myself another second if didn't come over immediately and say hello."

Colette looked at Jason with her big, beautiful hazel eyes. and said,

"I'm glad you did come over. I'm Colette Abraham, and *I* noticed *you,* standing over there."

She smiled and so did Jason.

"I know you've come out with your friends, and it would be rude of me to interrupt your evening. However, at the risk of sounding forward, I'd like to ask you two questions if I may."

Colette was pleased with this encounter and looked forward to the questions. She wondered what this handsome man could possibly want to ask her.

"You may." Colette responded.

With curious eyes, she watched him. She also wondered if she heard an accent. Confidently Jason began.

"Number one – are you in a serious relationship? And if you're not, my second question is – may I call you tomorrow?"

Colette was not surprised by his inquiries and answered the questions openly.

"No Jason English, I am not in a relationship at all right now. And to answer your second question, yes, you may call me tomorrow. I would be delighted to hear from you again."

Jason smiled, feeling proud because met someone like Colette. He seemed relieved as she offered him her personal card. It only included her first name and her telephone number. She handed the card to Jason and with a twinkle in her eyes said,

"I look forward to hearing from you tomorrow."

Colette had personal cards made to avoid mixing business with pleasure. This was perfect!

Jason graciously accepted the card. Before he placed it in the front pocket of his loose-fitting linen slacks, he scanned the card. Pleased, he looked at Colette and said,

"Thank you very much. I will call you tomorrow."

Jason looked directly into her eyes before he turned around and walked back to the other side of the room. Something stirred in Colette.

The tasting was getting crowded and now it was a challenge for Colette to see Jason. She believed that might be for the best because for some reason she couldn't keep her eyes off him.

"What did he say?" Lauren asked.

"That was kind of quick, wasn't it?"

Pamela was attentive as Colette answered,

"No. It was perfect. He's a gentleman, and now I really like him. We're going to talk tomorrow. I'll keep you posted."

There was a newfound lightness about Colette since speaking with Jason English. She wondered what the universe was bringing her. Eyes sparkling, heart opened and feeling soothed, Colette picked up one of the glasses of red wine, a Syrah, and proposed a toast.

"To newfound love."

And the three friends brought their glasses together.

When Colette was at home in bed that night she began reviewing the evening. She thought it was nice going up toward LA. She thought it was a great idea and she'd like to venture out more often. She continued thinking about Jason English. She liked the name, the voice, the face, and the body, or what she could imagine of it. She started remembering their brief conversation and she was almost certain she heard a Southern drawl. It was sexy. For some reason, she didn't feel the need to play cat and mouse with this guy. She said exactly what she was thinking when she said she would be delighted to hear from him again. There was something about Jason English. The next morning, Colette awakened naturally and lay in bed with her eyes closed, claiming her day. But today she felt excited. She felt like it was Christmas. Jason English was going to call her. She got out of bed and walked over to her meditation chair and closed her eyes.

Once Colette got home from work, she took off her clothes and put on a pair of jeans, canvas flats and a loose, oversized top. She walked into the kitchen and opened the refrigerator when her phone rang. She picked it up.

"Hello."

"Hi. Colette?" said the voice on the other end.

"This is Jason English. I hope I didn't catch you at a bad time." Jason waited to hear her response.

"No, no" Colette said with composure.

"This is a great time. I'm just in the kitchen searching for a snack of some sort. I'm starving."

"Really?" Jason said. He had an idea.

"I know this may seem hasty, but do you have plans for this beautiful Friday evening?" He asked.

Colette smiled to herself, thinking she hasn't had a date in quite some time.

"No Jason English, I do not have plans for this beautiful Friday evening. What's on your mind?"

"Well ..." Jason replied,

"I would love to take you to dinner tonight and have a proper introduction."

There was a brief silence before he continued,

"Would you like to have dinner with me tonight, Colette Abraham?"

Without hesitation, Colette answered.

I would love to have dinner with you tonight Jason English."

She couldn't remember a time when she'd felt so comfortable with someone. It was as if Colette had known Jason all her life. *Interesting*, she thought, as Jason suggested they have dinner in Long Beach at a restaurant called Michael's.

"The restaurant specializes in Italian food and is located in Naples. Are you familiar with it?" he asked.

"Very familiar." Colette said.

"Michael's, 555 on Ocean and Linden, and The Boathouse on the Bay are my favorite restaurants in Long Beach."

"Wonderful!" Jason responded with excitement.

"I'll make reservations for, how about 8 o'clock?"

"Perfect! I can meet you there."

Colette thought that would be best, since she doesn't really know Jason. And even though she believes he's the guy for her, she's smart.

"That's fair" Jason responded. He would have much rather picked her up, the way gentlemen do. And being from the South, Columbia, South Carolina, to be exact – his grandfather is going to die when he hears of this.

"I'll see you at Michael's."

Smiling, Colette closed her refrigerator door and trotted into her bedroom. She walked into her closet and went directly over to her green Theory pants. She had recently purchased a silk, billowy sleeved blouse. It looked like white canvas painted with big floral arrangements. She reached up and pulled a shoe box that housed her green silk Olivia Rose Tal mules. The green and orange pompoms on the front of the shoes made them flirty. Showering and dressing, Colette began to think of how much she likes this guy and what a gorgeous night to have dinner at Michael's. Perfect!

Colette arrives at Michael's and parks her car in the little strip mall next to the restaurant. She walks in the glass door and sees Jason at the bar. He stands as she walks over. The distance from the door to the bar is very short. Jason motions to an empty bar chair next to him. Colette walks directly up to Jason, he gives her a warm embrace and kisses her on the cheek. The embrace lasted a little longer than one would think from a stranger, before they took their seats at the bar. Jason has made reservations for dinner, but the table won't be ready until 8:15.

"Would you like a cocktail before dinner?" Jason asks Colette.

"Yes," she politely replies.

"I think I'll have a Bombay and St. Germain."

The bartender notices they're ready to order and walks over to them and asks what's their pleasure.

"One Bombay and St. Germain martini for the lady, and a Bombay and tonic for me" Jason says.

He turns and looks at Colette, who's looking at him. Their eyes lock. The arrival of the cocktails interrupt the spell. Slightly startled, Colette thanks the bartender. Jason picks up his glass,

"To a wonderful surprise. Colette Abraham."

Blushing, Colette touches her glass to his and says,

"I too got an unexpected surprise, Jason English."

Both Colette and Jason share a warm, comfortable smile.

"Your table is ready Mr. English." The waiter shows them to their table. They both stand, Colette retrieves her handbag, and Jason motions for her to walk ahead of him as they head to their table. Once the two are seated, Jason says to Colette,

"What do you have a taste for?"

"I always enjoy the flatbreads here" she responds.

"Would you like to start with that, a great bottle of wine and then check out the menu?" Jason asks.

"That sounds great. Do you prefer red or white?" she inquires, with the hope he enjoys a bold, jammy red.

"I love red wine" Jason says.

"I'm partial to big, bold fruit forward reds."

"So, we may have a similar pallet when it comes to wine. You've just recited my preference. Do you ever drink whites?" Colette adds.

"Only if it's a Viognier, or a few of my special ones from France." Jason says.

They're a bit fruit forward as well, yet not sweet." Colette smiles.

"What?" Jason asks with mischief.

"Those are my favorites too; not sure about the ones from France though. This is interesting." She raises an eyebrow and they begin to laugh.

Excited to know more about Colette, Jason asks,

"Where is it that you call home?"

"Huntington Beach; born and raised. And you?" she asks.

"You're looking at a proud Southern gentleman. I'm from Columbia, South Carolina. My mother and father are both from the South. They met at a football game while they were in college."

With that said, the waiter brings the flatbread, which is sliced into six pieces, and a beautiful bottle of red wine. After he uncorks the wine he pours a small amount into Colette's large sexy glass for her to taste. She holds her glass by its stem and swirls the wine in its bowl. She places her nose in the glass before she has a sip.

"Very nice."

She directs her compliment to the waiter, then looks at Jason and says,

"A lovely choice."

Jason smiles, saying,

"I'm glad you like it."

Before he walks away, the waiter fills Colette's glass, then Jason's. They take a sip of the wine and the two begin eating the flatbread. Colette is really hungry. She finishes her entire first piece before she says to Jason,

"I was really hungry."

She takes her napkin off her lap and daintily taps the corners of her mouth. Replacing her napkin, she continues,

"The spice in the wine pairs well with the peppers in this flatbread."

Jason gives her a look of curiosity and says,

"Yes, it does."

Grilled Scallops with Provence Herbs De Provence

Fresh scallops (as many as desired)

Fresh tarragon

Salt and white pepper

Oil scallops

Season scallops

Grill on medium heat until no longer pink serve

Three

SOUTHERN CALIFORNIA - JANUARY 2010
PLANS

*J*ason walks through the Air France terminal at Los Angeles International Airport. He goes through customs and is surprised at how quickly he's completed the usually arduous process. Briskly making his way to baggage claim and waiting for his luggage, he begins dialing Dave, one of his two best friends. The call connected.

"Hey man!" said the voice on the other end of Jason's Android cellphone.

"I hope you're at the curb," Jason laughs.

"I've had my share of airports for awhile."

"I'm not outside, but I am making my way past Southwest Airlines. If you remember, it's the first terminal." Dave said.

"I'll be there in a second," He assured Jason.

Jason spots his luggage and manages to get both of his bags and wheels them outside to wait for Dave. The warm air greets him and he remembers how much he's missed LA. The weather is just gorgeous and it's January. *Man!* Jason looks around at all the people coming and going. He's happy to be back on L.A. soil. A black Audi pulls up and Dave and James both get out of the car. They rush over to Jason and embrace him.

"Hey Jay!"

It is obvious all three men are really glad to see each other. James begins,

"You didn't put on any pounds, man over there in Paris eating great food and drinking fabulous wines! How was it?"

"Okay, okay," Dave interrupts in a jovial manner, "the man has been away studying and cooking at Le Cordon Bleu. I, or should I say we, expect the best meal ever!"

"Along with the best reds on the market," James says with a proud smile.

Happy they're back together again and really feeling good that Jason is making his dream a reality. Dave and James put Jason's bags in the trunk of the car, and they all get inside and head to Manhattan Beach.

In the car, Jason breaks the silence.

"What do you guys think about going to the club and shooting some hoops. I feel pretty rusty."

"Sounds good to me James?" Dave says.

Before James agrees with the plan he asks Jason if he's sure that'll be a good idea.

"Don't try to worm your way out of this man. I need to reacquaint you with me and my skills," Jason playfully says.

"You asked for it my friend." James says, and with that Dave begins the interrogation.

"So what was your culinary training like over there? Was it anywhere close to what you imagined it would be?"

Before Jason can answer the questions, James jumps in.

"I want to hear about the hotties you met in France. That's the juice."

Jason laughs, pleased to be back home and with his two most favorite people.

"I'll reply the quick and dirty way. First with *great*, then *yes* and, lastly *no time*. James, let me clue you in to a few things my friend. When a man is involved in his creative process, that *is* the hottie. No man, I didn't have time to look for sex or love. I was on a mission. Right now, food is my passion."

"Well what was the highlight of France for you?" James asked.

"Food and wine," Jason replies.

"Really man, there was no time to scout women when I was at Le Bleu." Jason looks at Dave.

"Now answering your questions. Culinary training in Paris was amazing! I met world- renowned chefs, saw the most beautiful country sides of France and drank and dined with the best of them. I had no idea I was in for such an incredible experience. I tell you guys, that was the quickest 365 days of my life."

Both Dave and James are thrilled by Jason's enthusiasm. They are pleased he has returned to the fold. With that feeling, they drive the rest of the way to his house in silence.

The sleek black Audi pulls up in front of a simple Craftsman home. It looks to be the ideal place for Jason. He unfolds his 6' 3" slender frame from the front of Dave's car and stretches his long body.

"Man, that feels good." He says as he begins bringing his knees to his chest to stretch even more.

"Okay you guys, are we sticking to the plans of the day?" Jason asks.

"Sticking with the plans?" Dave echoes.

"Don't think you're getting out of shooting some hoops, man. I still owe you an ass kicking from last year. It's time to make you pay up!"

All the guys start laughing and Dave tells Jason they'll give him time to unpack and take care of his particulars. James asks Jason,

"What time do you want to meet us on the basketball court Jay? Are we going to take the drive down to Horney Corner?"

"I've been flying for over nine hours. I know one of you is planning on driving, especially if we're not going to the athletic club," Jason replies to James.

"I got this," Dave says to Jason.

"No worries. Where do you want to play?"

Jason would rather save the LBC for another time and go to a place where he can sit in the sauna and get in the jacuzzi. His muscles are tight and he just wants to relax. After the emotional drain of packing and uprooting one year of his life, a huge farewell party at Alain Passard's restaurant, Arpege in the 17 arrondissement, and the long, yet comfortable flight back to the South Bay, Jason needs to sit in a hot body of water.

"You guys, I'd really rather just stay local and head over to the club once I spend a little time reacquainting myself with home" Jason says to his friends.

Dave and James look at one another with relief and respond,

"The athletic club it is."

Having just walked into his house after a year's absence, Jason stands in the living room and looks at his place. It's complete with furnishings, but it feels empty – almost lonely. He begins to think about the last time, he's been a serious relationship. He looks at his couch and thinks that it's just a couch, nothing special. Before he lets himself get too deep in his thinking, he brushes off the thoughts and, the direction they're going and grabs his bags, one at a time and takes them into his bedroom. Thank goodness, he had the sense to have his housekeeper come over and pick up his mail and maintain his house while he was gone. His bed is freshly made with his favorite sheets and Jason thinks he can't wait to get in and have a good night's sleep.

Jason kneels down and unzips one of his bags to begin unpacking. He looks at what he sees, and imagines all of France on the floor and changes his mind. At that moment, he decides to have his housekeeper come over at her earliest convenience and do that for him. He calls her.

"Elizabeth? It's me, Jason. Yes, I just got home."

Smiling at what he's hearing from her he continues,

"Thank you so much for taking such good care of my place while I was away. Yes, it's good to be home. I brought you a little something back."

Jason felt a little embarrassed when he said it so, and followed up with,

"It's no big deal."

Practically blushing, he adds,

"I was wondering if I could trouble you to come over and unpack for me when you have a chance?"

Jason sets it up with her to come by that day. Fortunately, today is Sunday and Elizabeth is off, but more importantly, because she loves Jason like she would a son if she had one. He finds his gym clothes and gets dressed. He gets his phone and calls Dave.

"Hey man."

When Dave picks up he says,

"Ready to be picked up? I can be out of here in five."

"No, I've decided to meet you guys there. I feel like getting behind the wheel of *The Rover*. I'll see you guys there in about 30 minutes."

Jason's made plans to continue documenting recipes today and scouting locations for a space for his new venture. It's best he drives to handle his business and not get distracted.

He ends the call, picks up his gym bag, walks through the kitchen and opens the door, which adjoins the house to his garage. Walking over to his vehicle, which is a steel-gray Range Rover, Jason opens the door on the driver's side. He tosses his bag inside and then gets behind the wheel. He wiggles his body around to adjust himself in the driver's seat to reacclimate with the feel of his Range Rover. Jason smiles and quietly sighs, "yeah." He looks in the console and sees that the keys are there and the tank is full of fuel. He thinks to himself, *I just love Elizabeth*. Jason reaches over his visor and opens the garage. Ready to go, he starts the car and lets it run for a bit. He sits there and his thoughts start to wander back to his empty house.

When Jason pulls into the parking structure he parks his car on the first level, gets his gym bag and heads toward the gym's entrance. Standing directly in front waiting for him is James and Dave. They begin to joke and talk smack about whose better than whom on the court. The three walk in and head straight over to the basketball courts. The guys are pleasantly surprised the courts are empty and they walk in with gym bags and all. Jason goes to the counter and gets two balls. Dribbling, and with swag, he trots onto the court calling the guys out.

"Okay, I know you don't want any of this!" he begins.

"So how do you want to play it since there are only three of us?"

"I think you may just want to shoot some hoops and not compete right away since you've been away playing in the kitchen," James chuckles.

"And I'm going to make you eat those words really soon my friend" Jason rebuts.

Then they all start running the court doing warmup exercises. The echoing sound of rubber soles and shellacked wooden floors send them to memories of their college years. They all attended the same college, USC, the University of South Carolina. James earned his master's degree in architecture. After working for a large company in Los Angeles, he recently started his own firm, EJM Architecture and Design. Dave majored in theater and currently works as a character actor in Hollywood. He's the guy who's not the star, but is always working. Jason majored in business and promised himself he would pursue his passion once he established himself as savvy businessman. His passion being food, Jason made the decision to go to Paris to study at Le Cordon Bleu. He wanted to really prepare himself before he launched his first restaurant.

The guys went down memory lane, discussing Columbia, South Carolina. They talked about Five Points, an area in Columbia where college students frequent. The bar they went to the most was Goat Feathers, right around the corner from one of Jason's favorite stores, the Gourmet Shop.

"I always hoped they would put a Dean & DeLuca somewhere in Columbia. Last I've heard, they never did. People still have to go all the way to Charlotte or New York to find one," Jason says.

"But I never mind taking a trip to The City. Such great places to eat."

He finishes his rant, when Dave chimes in.

"We must admit that Charleston has some nice restaurants too. Remember when we had those amazing Grilled Scallops with Provence Herbs De Provence? Great food is all over the South. Let's give it its props."

"You're right, I'm just thinking about how difficult it was when we were students to get what I was interested in" Jason says.

"Yeah," James agrees.

"I'm still surprised you are so fit considering the fact that you're a foodie. That's got to take some discipline."

Key Lime Pie - Emeril Lagasse

1 1/2 cups graham cracker crumbs
1/2 cup granulated sugar
4 Tbsp. (1/2 stick butter) melted
2 (14-ounce) cans sweetened condensed milk
1 cup key lime or regular lime juice
2 whole large eggs
1 cup sour cream
2 Tbsp. powdered sugar
1 tablespoon lime zest

Four

Colette and Jason panting, exhale in unison. They lay on the kitchen floor exhausted and sweaty. Most of what was on the island found its way next to them on the kitchen floor during their passionate tussle. Jason looks at Colette and she stares into his eyes, as if looking for his soul. *Where have you been?* she wonders; and in a whisper she says,

"Welcome back."

Jason smiles warmly and reaches for her hand. They lift themselves from the kitchen floor, picking up the vegetables that fell, and place them in the sink. Colette looks at Jason,

"Do you feel that?"

"Yes, I do. I knew we'd be okay for tonight."

The air conditioner is back on and all seems to be right with the world.

"We'd better hop in the shower and get a move on it," Jason insists.

"The clock says we have about six hours to pull it all together." Colette agrees.

"Do you want to start preparing the quail dish, while I start preparing the appetizers?" she asks.

"Yeah" he answers and walks over to the refrigerator.

"I've got everything for the Lobster Thermidor at the restaurant. The jumbo scallops are there as well. I'll call and have Val bring everything over once I've completed the quail sauce. It won't take much time."

"Good job" Colette says.

"I want to get everything ready for the scrumptious cocktails. I'm thinking I'll cut the fruit and citrus, and juice that's needed and refrigerate it to have it all ready for the bartenders. What do you think?"

"I think great-that's a good idea," Jason says.

The things that seem small are the important intricacies.

"Let's get started, darlin'. Six hours go by fast"

Jason says as he transitions into chef mode. Colette's worked with him a few times catering events so she knows what he expects. Jason gets supper serious at times like this. He asks Colette to read the menu to him again. She begins by reciting the structure of the evening and reading each dish aloud.

"Cocktail hour will begin the evening. Three fruity favorites will be served. Number one is made of fresh pomegranate juice, fresh squeezed blood oranges, top-shelf vodka, poured over ice. Number two is made of fresh muddled strawberries, simple syrup, top-shelf vodka with a sprig of mint, shaken and poured into a martini glass. The third one is fresh pineapple chunks soaked in vodka, pineapple-infused vodka, served very cold and poured into a cold martini glass. The classic cocktails will be served; gin and tonic or club soda, vodka and tonic or club soda, and classic martinis, and we can't forget the bourbon.

Appetizers:
Cheeses from France and Italy - soft and hard Fruit, baguettes and crackers (Colette is not certain when to serve the soup and salad so she Googles it and finds soup is served first and the salad can be after the meal. She wants this to be special so she decides she will serve the salad last, before desert.)

Soup
Simple flavorful broth
Cucumber
Cream fraiche

Main Course:
Quail in Rose Petal Sauce
Lobster Thermidor
Grilled scallops with fresh tarragon
Roasted Fingerling Potatoes with olive oil, sea salt, crushed black pepper and sprigs of rosemary
Brussels sprouts and garlic sautéed in olive oil.
Blanched asparagus with white wine and lemon served chilled with shaved parmesan.

Salad:
Freshly sliced fennel, thinly sliced onion and cherry tomatoes, chopped kale, dressed, with apple balsamic vinegar and organic Spanish olive oil.

Dessert
Flourless Chocolate Cake
Key Lime Tarts/made from the pie recipe
Strawberries with Grand Marnier, a dollop of fresh whipped cream and a sprig of mint

After dinner drinks:
Port
Sweet white dessert wine
Coffee
Finished with her presentation, Colette takes a bow as if she's just performed in a play.

"And for the grand finale," Jason sings,

"a big, beautiful Devil's Food birthday cake, with cream cheese frosting, decorated as a theater stage with curtain opening. I'm having it made at Derrick's."

With that said, he walks over to the Bose speaker and attaches his iPod. Amy Winehouse's voice booms the lyrics, "Why don't you come on over Valerie?"

Blanched Asparagus

Blanched Asparagus

In white wine and lemon

Served chilled

Shaved parmesan

Season to taste

Five

LONG BEACH, CALIFORNIA, 2010
APHRODISIAC

Jason and Colette are enjoying their first date.

"How is everything?" the waiter asks as he stands by Jason's side pouring wine into his glass. Appearing startled Jason answers,

"Oh, everything is fine, thank you."

The waiter adds,

"Are the two of you ready to order or do you need a little more time?"

Jason tells him they'll need just a few more minutes.

"We haven't even looked at the menu."

He looks at Colette, who is again, looking at him. The waiter tells them to take their time and he walks away. Colette and Jason pick up their menus and begin reading them.

"I really enjoy asparagus, but not tonight. I'm not sure if I'm going to have the Risotto Con Aragosta or the Scaloppine d'Anatra. Which entre are you considering?" Colette asks Jason.

"I'm having Tagliata Di Manzo. What about we order the Risotto and share it, that way you can still have room for the Scaloppine" Jason suggests.

"I like that." She goes on to say,

"I love risotto, yet I've never had it here."

"Neither have I" Jason says.

"Risotto, when prepared properly, is such a treat." She agrees with him as they sip their wine.

"So, Jason, what are you doing when you're not tasting wines in Manhattan Beach?" Colette asks as she engages him with a smile. Returning the smile, he says,

"I would usually be doing the day to day, working and being with my two buddies. But since I've just returned to the States Sunday, I'm acclimating to being home. And you?"

"My days appear to be pretty similar to yours, excluding the trip. I spend my days working. I have two best friends as well, Pamela and Lauren - we spend a lot of time together when I'm not working or creating personal projects," she says.

Jason then asks her what she does in her spare time.

"I like movies, the theater and classical music, but travel and great wines call my name."

She smiles again at Jason, but this time she is flirting. He flirts back.

"Oh really? I just got back from spending a year at Le Cordon Bleu in Paris. And traveling is one of my favorite pastimes. I'm going to refrain from inviting you to Quebec in May. Tomorrow might be better, when there's no wine involved."

Jason chuckles and gestures for the waiter. Before the waiter arrives, he confirms with Colette, by an exchange of expressions, that another bottle is in order. When the waiter does get to their table,

"Another bottle of the same" Jason says to him.

The two sit quietly for a few moments. They both feel the sweet effect of the delicious wine. Feeling relaxed and really comfortable with one another, Colette breaks the silence.

"I've yet to meet a man who is so much for me. It's astonishing."

The feeling between the two of them is warm. They look at one another. Jason hasn't felt this way in quite some time. He imagines the softness of her lips and wonders if they taste like candy. He gracefully lifts himself a few inches out of his seat. He leans toward her and says,

"May I?"

Then he kisses her. Colette returns his kiss and the waiter is back uncorking the second bottle.

Carnaroli rice with Maine lobster, leeks and cream is placed before them in a simple bowl.

"This risotto looks heavenly," Colette says as she reaches for her fork.

Jason agrees and without hesitation, as if it is something they normally do, they pick up their forks and begin to eat from the same dish. Immediately after the risotto is finished the waiter brings the main courses. Duck Scalloppine with Chestnuts and Heirloom Carrot Farrotto for Colette, and carved Prime New York Strip Steak with Cipollini Onions, Potato Gnocchi and Rosemary Reduction for Jason. The two sit comfortably and enjoy their meals. Talking and laughing, they say they are very happy to be the recipients of such a gift.

"I am so glad I decided to go to Tin Roof last night. I had no idea this would come of It."

He points a finger at himself and at her. They finish the second bottle of wine and the waiter offers them another. They both refuse and look at each other sheepishly.

"Another bottle of Pellegrino will be sufficient," Jason says to the waiter.

The waiter nods and quickly walks toward the kitchen. When he returns with the water he offers them dessert menus. Colette asks Jason,

"Would you mind sharing something else with me?"

"What's your desire?" he asks playfully. She replies,

"Torta Di Cioccalato. I love flourless chocolate cake with salted caramel and crispy prosciutto."

"Sounds delicious" Jason says to her.

"I make a mean flourless chocolate tart. I'd really enjoy preparing one for you one day, if that's okay."

"That sounds yummy. Anything involving chocolate is my friend." Colette says.

"So" Jason chuckles,

"I'll make a mental note that Ms. Abraham has a sweet tooth."

The check arrives and Colette and Jason exit Michael's. It must be about 11 p.m. When they get outside, the valet walks over and gives Jason his keys. Jason hands him $20. The car is now on Second Street awaiting its owner. Jason takes his keys and asks Colette if she'd like to take a stroll around Naples. She tells him a walk will be nice.

"Would you mind if I hold your hand?" Jason asks her.

"I would love it if you held my hand," she says.

Jason holds his hand out for Colette to take. She reaches out and takes his hand. They walk down to the corner of Ravenna Drive and make a left. The couple strolls the Ravenna until they reach Rivo Alto Canal. Jason decides to take Colette to the set of stairs that lead down to the sidewalk to the canal, which unfolds in front of beautiful spacious homes, and myriad-sized boats, which are docked on the beautiful canal. They find themselves walking past the huge houses perched on the water in front of boat slips. Colette notices a house that has a sign in the window that reads, "A spoiled rotten dog lives here." She thinks it's sweet and shows Jason. They continue to walk down the canal, looking at the boats and the homes. Both are in their own reveries, imagining life in the best of worlds. Thinking about how beautiful it is here tonight.

"It's beautiful here tonight," Colette says to Jason.

"I've haven't been here before."

"I've been here for the Long Beach Boat Parade and the Naples Island Holiday Lights Walk. It is so beautiful" Jason responds.

They continue to walk in silence and their thoughts begin to shift. It's now well past 11:30 and Colette is thinking about how she can drive her car home. She doesn't want to leave her car and come back again tomorrow. Jason wonders what this is all about – his feelings for this woman he's met at a wine tasting last night. Jason stops and stands in front of Colette.

"I don't mean to be forward. I've already asked your permission to dinner tonight, and to kiss you. I don't feel the need to play games or anything of that nature. I want to ask you if you'll go out with me again on Sunday afternoon to The Getty in Malibu."

Colette is happy Jason is saying this to her. She is feeling the same way about him.

"I will go out with you again on Sunday, Jason. As I told you yesterday, I'm not in a relationship. And I will add – I like you Jason English."

Jason is thinking about how wonderful this night has been. He's also thinking about the wine they've consumed. Once their walk is completed, Jason suggests they use a service that sends someone to drive your car home and someone to drive you home. Jason was made privy to this information when he was living in France.

"Let's sit in one of our cars while I make the call."

Jason taps the numbers on his phone. After he ends the call he tells Colette they will have to wait about 10 to 15 minutes before the service arrives. They're booth spinning from the whirlwind of emotions between them. They sit quietly and wait.

When the cars arrive, Jason walks over to one of the them and gives his credit card information to the driver and informs him that he's taking care of both services. Colette is talking to the other guys, giving them her address. Jason walks over to the car Colette is entering and asks her if she's okay. He then asks her to,

"Please call me as soon as you're safe inside your house. How long should it take them to get you there?"

"I'm only about 15 minutes away, if it takes that long" she answers.

"So, I'll hear from you soon," Jason says. He gives her a little peck on the lips and watches her get in the car, closes her door and walks over and gets into the car that's driving him to Manhattan Beach.

Colette gets home in about 15 minutes. She is so happy her car is in her garage and she didn't have to leave it in Long Beach. She thinks to herself, *I like that service*. She takes her cellphone out of her purse and calls Jason. When he answers, she says,

"Mr. English, I'm in my living room."

He was still being driven home when he received her call.

"Well that is music to my ears," a delighted Jason responds.

There's a slight pause before he says,

"Thank you so much for tonight. I had a great time with you. I would have never imagined my first week being back in the States would include such a gift."

"Me too. Thank you for inviting me to dinner." Colette says.

"I'm really looking forward to Sunday. There's an interesting mythological exhibit beginning Sunday. Are you interested in Greek mythology?"

"Absolutely. I studied mythology my freshman year at Vanguard. I love the story of Psyche and Eros. I pay attention to the way mythology plays out in every culture that currently exists. It's fascinating – not that everyone believes that to be true," Colette says.

"I tend to watch the world through the eyes of someone quite curious," Jason says.

"Curious enough to venture on the side of possibilities and probabilities, rather than to allow fear and shallow thinking to disconnect me from the vastness of all there is."

"That's exciting. We have lots to discuss" responds Colette. Then she says,

"Well handsome, I'm going to bid you farewell and take my little self to bed. I really enjoyed myself with you and I'm looking forward to Sunday."

"I won't keep you up any longer. Get your rest and I too, look forward to Sunday. Good Night, Colette."

Colette says good night to Jason and they end the call.

Roasted Fingerling Potatoes

Potatoes (enough for your guests)

Olive oil

Salt

Pepper

Rosemary sprigs

Bake until tender

Six

Manhattan Beach, January 2010
Cocktail Hour

The guys turn in the basketballs. They're drenched in perspiration and breathing heavily after strenuous balling. They go into the locker room and finally put their belongings in a locker.

"Let's hit the showers and head to the sauna," James suggests.

"Great," Dave and Jason agree.

"Then the jacuzzi" Jason says.

"I can't wait to soak and relax my weary bones."

"Yeah" Dave says.

"Let's go to Petros afterward and have some dinner. I'm guessing you'll appreciate something from a region other than France."

"I would" Jason assures him.

"Greek will be good."

Famished at this point, the guys sit in the Jacuzzi and plan what they're going to eat for dinner tonight. Jason starts to recite various specialties he's had at Petros. They finally quiet down and relax. They soak and Jason is so pleased. His tired muscles are soothed and he feels rejuvenated. The jacuzzi has given him a second wind. Jason asks the guys,

"What's up for this week? Is anything happening that we should attend?"

"Funny you should ask, James says.

"There's a wine tasting at Tin Roof on Thursday night. I was thinking we should all go and you can start getting your beach legs back."

"Manhattan Beach has missed you man," Dave chimes in.

"Me, on the other hand," James says,

"I want to go and see if there's anyone interesting out there."

They all laugh, and Jason adds,

"Here we go again. It's like I never left."

The guys hit the showers and then head to their lockers. While dressing, Jason takes the conversation to a more serious level and begins to discuss relationships.

"James, when are you ever going to settle down man? Does that even interest you right now?" Jason asks.

"That's a good and fair question," James replies.

The tone has shifted and it's welcomed. The good thing is these three have always been able to be candid with each other. They've never had to play games or be disingenuous in their friendships. James continues,

"I don't know. Sometimes I feel a bit afraid to take the serious plunge. I know it may sound wussy, but man, I don't feel like having drama or heartache. You know what I mean?"

"I know what you mean man, but those are the risks we must take to find what we want out there. I would have never met Karen if I didn't decide to dive in," Dave shares.

"I know," James says.

After a slight pause he carries on, saying,

"So – yes Jason. I plan on settling down one day, just not right now. What's with the serious talk? Have *you* met someone? You said that in France your hottie was the culinary arts - food and wine. Do I smell something cooking?"

"No, not really. It's just that when I got home and stood in my living room today, it, it just felt so empty. You know, like something was missing when I walked in the door. I can't explain it really."

"I think you are ready for a woman," Dave says.

He quickly corrects himself as not to be misunderstood, and says,

"Not like that. I think you're ready for YOUR woman."

All three men stand quietly, appearing to be deep in thought before Dave asks,

"Are we ready? Let's meet at Petros and have a fine meal and some cocktails. First round is on me!"

"Now you're talking!"

James says to Dave as they pick up their gym bags and walk to the parking structure.

*he ambiance is nice in Petros. It's loungey and inviting. The three friends walk up to the bar and take a seat. Dave then walks back over to the reservation area and places their name on the list. It's Sunday, and he's hoping they won't have to wait long since they didn't make reservations. Dave walks back over to the bar and takes a seat. A perky little female bartender approaches them.

"Hey fellas. What'll you have?"

Jason immediately answers,

"I'll have a Bombay Sapphire martini, straight up with three blue- cheese olives, if you will."

"I'd like a Chopin martini straight up, one olive" Dave says.

James asks the bartender,

"Give me your finest tequila. I think that'll be just what the doctor ordered."

The drinks arrive and Dave proposes a toast.

"To Jason, the other one of my best friends."

He glances over at James and says,

"Welcome home. And I'm speaking for both of us when I say, we're really glad that you're back."

"I love you guys," Jason replies.

*S*tanding at the island, Colette pulls the round cutting board toward her and gathers up the basket of fresh limes, strawberries and mint, while leaving the pineapples on the kitchen counter. She begins cutting the limes into wedges. Once that task is completed, she begins slicing the strawberries and picking fresh mint off its stems. She then removes a sauce pan from the cabinet and fills it with purified water and a few cups of granulated sugar. Colette places it on the gas stove and turns it on low and begins preparing the simple syrup. This is one of many tasks that she hopes to complete. After she's cut the limes, they're placed into a beautiful glass bowl and placed in the refrigerator. The mint is placed to rest in a glass bowl as well. Once the strawberries are sliced, she places them into a huge marble bowl accompanied by a matching muddler, so she can muddle them later. Now for the pineapples. Collette walks over to the counter to get the pineapples and lifts one of them in each of her hands. Walking back to the island, she thinks she should have done this a few days ago.

"Maybe I would have if I'd thought of it a few days ago" she mumbles to herself.

"Are you saying something, darlin'?" Jason asks.

Colette replies,

"Yes. I was saying to myself that if I had been thinking, I would have soaked the pineapple cubes in the vodka a few days ago."

"Yeah," Jason responds.

"But they'll still have a nice subtle flavor of the vodka. Don't worry. This is going to be a spectacular gathering."

"I know sweetheart. Are you excited?" she asks.

"Certainly I am. Baby-Girl is 30 years old today. I can't believe it."

Jason is reflective and smiles at his thoughts.

"I like the fact that we've only invited 20 guests." Jason says.

"Me too" Colette says.

"That'll keep it more intimate, allowing Janis to spend quality time with all of them. Not to mention, 20 guests fit comfortably in our house."

Jason begins to laugh and Colette joins him.

Colette and Jason are in the kitchen working together, they move and sway like dancers on a stage. They've managed to get it all together for the party tonight. The tasks are complete. Jason called Val and she's brought the Lobster Thermidor and the scallops from the restaurant. The rosemary fingerling potatoes smell delicious – one of Jason's favorites. With pride, the couple acknowledge that all the work is done; everything's ready for the bartenders, and the birthday cake is on its way. They survey the spotless kitchen when Jason says,

"I think it's time for a martini." He walks over to the bar and gets the Bombay Sapphire vodka and two huge martini glasses. He asks Colette,

"Dirty or straight?" She tells him,

"Make mine a little dirty with three, please."

Jason makes the cocktails and the two of them take their Martinis and walk in the direction of their bedroom to get dressed for the party. Once in the bedroom, Jason walks up to Colette, removes her drink from her hand and says,

"I can't believe we've got an hour on our side."

She smiles at him.

The tables are set with beautiful wine glasses, china and the finest silver. Colette loves little lights, and they're illuminating the house, offering a festive ambiance. The bartenders and servers are there preparing for the evening. They're dressed elegantly in black and white.

Jason is in the living room listening to Carla Bruni when the doorbell rings. He is wearing a Davy's gray, casual silk suit, a white silk shirt with white-gold and black onyx cufflinks. His shoes are black lamb skin loafers. The living-room ceilings are high with clean lines. The windows are large and plenty, offering generous natural light in the daytime hours. The walls are painted cool white to match the white furnishings and window treatments.

Color is peppered throughout the room, assisting the home with its exhibition of sophistication and fun.

The front door gives the illusion of floor-to-ceiling French doors. As Jason walks across the room, responding to the bell, Colette walks out of the bedroom to join him.

"You are so beautiful,"

Jason says to the women he loves more than anything. She's wearing a sleeveless, fitted, Davy's gray, Azzedine Alaia sheath dress that stops directly below her knees. There is a kick split in the back giving her room to move. She's wearing red silk Oscar de la Renta shoes, chunky David Yurman jewelry, a white-gold necklace, matching bracelet, and a ring on her right middle finger. Her nails are short and smart, painted in her favorite red color to match her red lipstick. Colette has decided to wear her curls in a loose pile on the top of her head, cascading around her soft, caramel colored face. Her hazel eyes are displaying mascara and a hint of gray eye shadow. She is a picture of perfection!

Jason opens the door and greets David and Karen, their first guests. The couple walks inside. They've been dating since Los Angeles. Even though the guys are good friends, Colette and Karen are just getting to know each other. James has informed the guys he will not be attending this function, which is unusual for him. James usually makes every important event and Janis is going to be really, disappointed. David lives here in Columbia now. Although he is an actor and works primarily in Los Angeles, he also works out of Atlanta, Georgia, when he's not on location. He has recently moved back to Columbia because he wants to raise his future children in a place that's conducive to family life. He and Karen have been talking about their future and marriage and agree on the idea of raising children in the South, which made the move easy for her.

Colette and Karen walk over to the other side of the room to give the guys a bit of privacy.

"It's so good to see you, Karen. How've you been?"

"I've been pretty good. Columbia is so much different than I'd imagined."

"Is that good or bad?" Colette asks.

Karen tells her that she really likes it, yet David has been a little concerned that she may not be able to handle the change.

"I'm so glad you are happy here! Have you considered what you're going to do for work?" Colette asks her.

"No. I haven't thought about it yet. We've been traveling a lot, back and forth to L.A. I do need to think about it though," Karen says.

Then she asks Colette what she does in Columbia for work. Colette says,

"When I initially arrived, I was doing consulting for the insurance firm I worked for in L.A. When I ended that, I began consulting here in Columbia for another insurance firm."

"Is that what you're doing now?" Karen asks her with deep curiosity.

"No, it's not," Colette says.

"Six months ago I opened an interior design firm; CE Abraham Interiors. I'm in the marketing phase."

"That's amazing," Karen says.

"How long have you been interested in interior design?"

"I've been interested in fashion and design since I was a little girl," Colette answers.

"After having been here for a while, I can say Columbia has been quite welcoming."

Once the ladies walk away from Jason and David, David says to Jason,

"I don't know what's going on with James. His call yesterday, about not coming to the party was so ominous. I did not expect it."

"Well, man, we'll see what it's all about after tonight because the party is the topic of the day. Janis is the focus. I'm so proud of her. The final completed draft of her first off-Broadway play! Man, that's unbelievable. My little sister turned 30 years old today. I keep tearing up just thinking about it. I can remember when she was just a little girl." Jason says.

David looks at him and squeezes his arm,

"Tonight is going to be phenomenal! Look at this place. Did you and Letty (Colette's nickname) do all of this yourselves?" Jason responds,

"Yes, we did. It was a good bonding project too man."

"Good for you Jason. I know how you can shut down and get into your own head. You've got to communicate that to Letty and assure her it has nothing to do with her." David suggests.

Jason thinks about how he's going to explain his moods. David doesn't even know why he's been this way. He can't figure out why he's never told her – or mentioned it to David and James.

"Thanks David. I believe tomorrow at brunch I'll explain a little bit more about myself to Mrs. English."

Jason begins to think about what happened between him and Suzette when he was in Paris without Colette. *Why have I kept this from her? I didn't accept her advances after the first kiss. …* Jason is questioning his own secrecy.

Colette and Karen realize the guys are walking over and they prepare to receive them graciously. Before the guys reach them Colette asks Karen if she'd like to have lunch on Tuesday. She thinks this will be a good time to finally get more acquainted with her. Karen agrees to meet Colette at Motor Supply Company Bistro on Gervias (pronounced-Jervai) Street in the Vista, on Tuesday at noon.

Getting acquainted

Karen walks through Carol Saunders jewelry store, which is connected to Motor Supply Company. She begins browsing through the jewelry and the art. When Colette walks in the store, she notices Karen is intensely looking at pieces in the fine jewelry section. As Karen looks at the gold and diamond rings, Colette walks up to her with a radiant smile and says,

"You hungry?"

"Famished," Karen replies as if Colette has been there all along.

She turns away from the jewelry and gives her attention to Colette and warmly embraces her.

"I haven't eaten anything yet. David had to rush off to L.A. this morning and I was up late helping him pack. He's not back until next week and I opted to stay here."

"Good girl, Karen. That's the best way to become acquainted with Columbia. There is so much here. Have you been on Devine Street for shopping yet? There are so many cute little stores on Devine." Karen says,

"No. I've only been in our neighborhood, Heathwood. I've been to L.A. so many times since we moved here, I haven't felt the urge to shop. But what are you doing after lunch?"

"Shopping with you on Divine," Colette sings.

"I need some time out too. Don't forget, I've been spending a lot of time preparing for that fantastic party you attended this weekend. I think something new is in order. Strolling down Divine will give me a chance to look at things and get ideas for my first project."

"When did you get your first project?" Karen inquires with excitement.

"I don't have one yet. But I just want to start keeping my eyes open for the first one. If I allow it, it will come into my sphere,"

Colette tells her. Then Colette says,

"So, let me ask you, Karen, has there been any conversation with David about really securing your future?"

There was a brief pause.

"If this is not a good topic let me know."

As Karen and Colette make their way toward the back of the store, through the door that leads to Motor Supply, Karen says,

"It is interesting I should walk into a jewelry store while looking for this restaurant; and as fate would have it I'd be in the gold and diamond ring section of Carol Saunders."

Colette quietly squeals with delight and then contains herself before asking,

"Does this mean David proposed?"

"Yes!" Karen answers.

She reaches out and takes Colette's hands. The two tap their feet and make little jumping motions. Her face is glowing as she continues.

"Yesterday. It was really early in the evening and we were outside on the patio having a light dinner when he asked me. We'd mentioned it before when we lived in L.A. – nothing ever came of it. But David is such a stand-up kind of guy, I knew this day would come."

"I think that's beautiful," Colette says.

"Jason and I have got to take the two of you out to celebrate this glorious occasion."

"That's sweet of you, Colette," Karen says.

The waitress is approaching them as they reach for the menus to make their choices. Karen notices the menus are handwritten.

"This is different, the menus being written by hand. I like it. It lends a splash of familiarity."

Colette agrees and they begin to read the menu. The waitress greets them pleasantly with a warm South Carolinian drawl.

"How y'all doin' this afternoon?" she asks.

"I'm Betty -Mae and I'll be serving you. Is this your first time at Motor Supply Company?"

Karen tells her it is her first time there and Colette lets her know she comes there often.

"Well then," Betty-Mae begins cheerfully,

"Let me start off by telling you our menus change each day, that's why they're handwritten. If there's something you think you might like, grab it now because it may not be on the menu for some time, if ever again."

She tells them the specials of the day and says,

"Take your time and look over the menu ladies. I'll check on you in a couple minutes."

Before she leaves their table, she inquires,

"Can I bring either of you a cocktail, a glass of wine or champagne?"

Colette takes the liberty and requests,

"A bottle of Veuve Clicquot please, and your finest champagne flutes!"

Karen's eyes sparkle and her smile exudes appreciation for such kindness.

"I'll get that right away." Betty Mae says, and then inquires,

"Is this a celebration of some sort, if I may ask?"

Colette flashes her radiant smile at Betty-Mae and says,

"Yes, ma'am it is. You see that lovely lady sitting across from me? She's getting married!"

"Congratulations!"

Betty-Mae says with excitement.

She's a pretty black girl, seemingly in her mid-20s. Almond-shaped brown eyes, long eyelashes, with a head full of hair that looks like lamb's wool contained by a fashionable headband, displaying her gorgeous face.

"Let me get that to y'all quick. This is great news. And again, congratulations!"

Betty-Mae dashes off and out of sight. Karen resumes the conversation.

She continues by talking about how she first met David. It was before attending, The Red Book Dialogues, at the Hammer Museum in Los Angeles in 2010. The dialogue that was of interest to her was a scheduled talk between Helen Hunt and James Hillman. She'd gone with some friends from Pacifica, her alma mater, to a party in Bel Aire. They were out in the backyard with other guests having appetizers and wine, discussing what they'd want to experience at the upcoming event at the Hammer Museum.

Karen walked away from her table to fetch some water and David was getting water as well. He was interested in listening to James Hillman, who has since made his transition but was phenomenal. Karen and David began to talk, and as they say, the rest is history.

Betty-Mae shows up with the bubbly. She sets the beautiful, sophisticated flutes down in front of Colette and Karen. She brings the bottle and an elegant champagne bucket to rest the Veuve Clicquot on ice. Betty-Mae skillfully opens the beverage without a sound and deftly fills each flute.

"Enjoy ladies. I'll be back to take your orders, unless you're ready to order now," Betty-Mae says.

"Thank you so much Betty-Mae. We'll get your attention when we're ready" Colette tells her.

The waitress nods in agreement and Colette raises her glass to Karen and says

"To Karen. May the life you make with David be as beautiful as the energy you emit."

Karen raises her glass and says,

"I too would like to make a toast. To Colette Abraham-English, a woman I am pleased to call my friend."

The women exchange sincere looks of a deep bond forming and take their first sip.

Lamb Kleftiko

- 6 garlic cloves
- 3 Tbsp. roughly chopped oregano
- 1 Tbsp. roughly hopped rosemary
- Zest 1 lemon
- Juice of 2 lemons
- ½ tsp ground cinnamon
- 3 Tbsp. olive oil
- 2 kg leg of lamb
- 1 kg Desiree potatoes/ half or quartered
- 5 bay leaves

Seven

The guys have had a great meal at Petros, and James is in the hot seat now. They've just ordered another round and they're really happy to be together again.

"So man," Jason says to James.

"let's continue our relationship conversation. You said earlier you didn't want to deal with pain. David told you that that's the risk we take when we want to have what we want. Let's peel back those layers to this fear."

"Jay," James responds.

"I really believe I won't be good at this. I think I'll be the one who's more invested than she will be."

"That's hard for me to imagine" David says.

"Unless that's why you never stay longer than a few months once you begin to date someone."

Dave says this as if he's just found the missing piece to a puzzle.

"Bingo!" James says to them.

Jason shoots back,

"So that means we're total opposites when it comes to matters of the heart. I'm excited to find that someone to figure 'it' out with. I want someone to love, no matter what the cost. You fellas don't know what I felt today walking into my house to a lot of nothingness. Being away for a year and coming home to a furnished house with no one in it to greet me. I'll take the pain that accompanies creating a wonderful life with someone, over spending my life alone any day."

David agrees with Jason.

"Where did you guys get the courage?" James asks.

"Ever since I've been dating, feeling something deeply for whomever it has been has scared the bejesus out of me. So, I decided a long time ago not to get caught up," James says.

Jason tells James how wonderful he thinks good relationships are.

"You know, in France I was privy to some relationships that were amazing. It was so nice seeing couples together – young and old. I'm ready to find someone. Just like David said earlier today," Jason says.

"I'm ready to find *my* woman. And now that we're discussing this, I realize that I am excited to go to that wine tasting at Tin Roof this Thursday night. I'm designating this Thursday night as my start date," Jason says.

"Your start date to be on the prowl?" James asks.

"No man," Jason answers.

"My start date of being open to Cupid's arrow."

Jason is smiling broadly now, almost as if he's found her already.

"I'm really glad to hear that, Jason." David says.

"Having a partner to share your life with is ineffable. There is nothing like it. Karen and I are new in our relationship. I met her the year before you left for Paris, but nothing really came it because of our schedules. But it was during that year we reconnected and it's gotten serious. Here it is 2010 and she's my girl. I often wonder how I lived that long without her. I know she's the one for me."

"I can't wait to meet her, David." Jason says.

"Oh, you will. I talk about you all the time," David tells him.

"She's a good one" James says, and then sits with them in a brief contemplative moment before adding,

"I'm really considering this, guys. But just thinking about it gives me the same feeling as the thought of skydiving, and you both know that's something I never want to do. I can just see myself going splat! - on the ground below – having jumped willingly to my own death."

Jason and David look at each other and they all begin to laugh heartily.

⌒➔

*J*ason pulls the Rover in his garage and walks through the door that leads to the kitchen. He drops his gym bag on the floor, which leads to the laundry room. He sighs a sigh of contentment that is full of appreciation.

"Wow," he says aloud to himself.

"Fresh off the plane, and hit the ground to this big day!"

He thinks it has been a good and informative day. *Learning about my desire to be in a relationship, learning David is in a serious relationship, and that James is terrified of being hurt. Wow.* He goes and grabs a bottle of alkaline water. He then walks into his bedroom, steps out of his shoes, takes off his shirt, takes off his trousers and gets in his inviting bed. He's thought about this bed many times throughout the year and now he's home again. He pulls the soft sheets over his body, arranges himself for comfort and drifts off to sleep.

Monday morning (4 a.m., Jason has jetlag). The house is fresh with flowers on the dining room table; a small touch from Elizabeth. She always tells him a man needs something soft in his home, and his life. If Jason doesn't have a woman, then he needs soft sheets and fresh, fragrant flowers. Jason smiles as he remembers the first time she said that to him. He never considered it before. But now Jason remembers how nice it is to have fresh flowers each week, and soft sheets that smell good. Agreeing with what she told him some time ago, he looks near the flowers and sees a sweet note from Elizabeth – *You shouldn't spoil me so. Thank you so much. I love them!* Jason gave her a gift of beautiful earrings, made in France with a matching bracelet and necklace. He smiles inside.

After enjoying a breakfast of coffee, an omelet of eggs, kale and cheese, Jason is feeling good to be back, and really excited to begin his new venture. In his office, sitting on his drafting table, Jason's briefcase contains copious notes that he looks over. Wanting to meet with James about his new space – once he locates one – Jason knows that James will design something unique for it.

The drafting table gives him the room to spread out and to stand if he likes. Sketching a rough draft to show James when they meet, Jason shifts his attention, and begins to look at menus, and recipes he created while in France. He's thinking about preparing dishes for people to sample his skills in the kitchen. So, he decides to have a gathering to see how people respond to his cooking. This is making him a little nervous. To clear his mind, Jason decides to take a run on the beach. He thinks better that way. Walking away from the drafting table, Jason goes into his bathroom and washes his face and brushes his teeth. He sees his cell and decides to leave it charging. *I don't want any distractions, not that I have someone interested in calling me right now. Not yet,* he thinks. Jason locates his running shoes and running garb and gets ready to head out.

After lacing up his shoes he's out the door, running toward the ocean. Jason's thoughts are swirling in his head. Every so often they're interrupted by the feeling of emptiness. He shakes it off and begins to focus on his new restaurant. He wants to have it in an area that is easy for residents to walk to. There's a potential location not far from houses on the Strand. Jason imagines couples walking out of their homes, onto the beach and directly to his restaurant.

"Yeah," he says quietly, as he wonders if that place is available, and if it is, what price is being asked for it.

I really like that spot, Jason says to himself as he begins to talk aloud.

"I can see all of the people enjoying my food, the environment, the music that's piped through the speakers, wafting in the atmosphere. What colors should it be? I've got to go look at colors pallets at Home Depot. Okay, that's where I'll go after my run."

Jason shuts it off and gets in the zone and runs as a gazelle. His long legs move effortlessly as they slice through the invisible elements. He's in the flow, as he runs on the Strand and then to the location he's considering for his new venture. He stops in front of the building and tries to peer through the papered-up windows. He can see a vast space with high, beamed ceilings. Lights are dangling as if someone took the decorations away. He struggles to see more, but it's impossible because the area he's looking through is so small. There's a sign barely noticeable in the left-hand corner of a side window. It's almost as if someone doesn't want this space occupied. Curious, Jason squats down to see what's written on the sign. There's a telephone number and the name Suzette.

"Hum," Jason says, as he memorizes the number.

He begins running toward Manhattan Beach Boulevard and back to his house, filled with inspiration and a head full of ideas.

Saturday morning Colette wakes up with Jason on her mind. After having such a magical time with him she's not surprised he's the first thought of her day. She had no idea she was going to meet someone she really likes. She lies in bed and recaptures the night. She thinks of Jason's face – his sexy cleft chin – his nice brown eyes – and his hands. She remembers what his hands felt like when they intertwined with hers as they walked along the canals of Naples. She thinks about how strong and big they are. Colette begins to wonder what he does to have such nice hands. She likes their olive color and size, and the way she felt when her hand was safely nestled inside of his. She sighs, closes her eyes and imagines Jason holding her hand.

The melody of her cellphone breaks her reverie.

"Hey Pamela," Colette says as she makes the sounds of someone stretching.

"I'm awake and just lying here enjoying not having to go to the office," she says.

Pamela, on the other end is asking her if she'd like to get coffee and perhaps go to Fashion Island, an upscale, outdoor mall in Newport Beach.

"Yep," Colette immediately replied.

"I've got lots to tell you."

The friends make plans to meet at Pamela's and head to Fashion Island for coffee and browse through the stores. Colette gets out of bed and decides she'll have to meditate later that day. She wants to be at Pamela's in 30 minutes, so she hurries to get in the shower. Hair in a ponytail on top of her head, she gets in.

Later, when Pamela opens the door to welcome Colette, she looks at her and gives her a suspicious stare.

"What?" Colette asks, with a smile so big and bright it competes with the sun.

"Don't give me that 'what?' business," Pamela says to her.

"Let's just get in the car and go to The Coffee Bean. We can have coffee there and then go shopping. Is that good?" Colette asks.

"Of course," Pamela says.

"I can't wait to hear what's behind the sunshine!"

They both laugh and Colette can't contain herself and starts talking. Walking out of the house toward Pamela's car, Pamela's cellphone chirps like birds singing. She taps her answer call button,

"Hey Lauren. Come join me and Colette for coffee and stories. Colette has news."

Colette's looking at Pamela enthusiastically, like she's about to burst. On the other end of the phone, Lauren's asking questions Pamela can't answer.

"We'll wait here for you sweetie. Just put a rush on it, because someone over here's like a piñata. One tap in the right place and all the goodies are going to come pouring out."

Pamela ends the call and looks at Colette endearingly and asks,

"Can you hold the story for another five minutes? You don't want to repeat it all, do you?"

Pamela thinks about it for a second and says,

"Well maybe you do since you are the storyteller."

Colette smiles at Pamela and says,

"Well she'd better hurry, because just breathing seems to make this little piñata want to let all the goodies out."

They laugh again and sooner than they expect the front door flies open.

"What have I missed?" Lauren asks.

She's wearing her brown hair up in a messy-cute ponytail, her Lululemon skinny workout pants and a matching razor-back top, and Prada flip-flops, as she has no intentions of going to yoga today. Lauren's anticipation is Colette's news, hoping she releases all the goodies – every single detail.

"Okay," Colette says, and they all walk to Pamela's car.

As they're going to the coffee shop, Colette starts telling her story from the beginning, the Friday night phone call. She's a master storyteller, as she always has one to tell. Colette's a "tell the details" kind of girl. From each look, breath, voice octave, and accent – if there's one she'll make an attempt to place you in the culture. Colette makes sure you feel like you're right there.

The girls are enraptured as Colette tells her story. They have questions, but are too engaged to interrupt her. Lauren and Pamela aren't in relationships and are so happy this is happening to their friend. About an hour has passed and coffee has been sipped, muffins have been nibbled and Colette has shared the goods. Once she's finished with her story they all sit silent. Lauren breaks the ice.

"This sounds like a fairy tale. I love it! It's so nice, right?"

She looks at Pamela, who agrees. They're both smiling.

"I knew you would finally meet the guy," Pamela says.

"You deserve this Colette. After spending so much time being unhappy in your career and working such long hours, a nice gentleman to spend time with is so nice."

"And he appears to really be a gentleman." Colette adds.

"It's about time someone is paying attention to you," Pamela continues.

"I know," Colette says.

"I'm not even going to worry about the normal things we women worry about. Things like, 'Should I like him this much so soon? Did he really mean that look he just gave me? Does he want more from me than I am willing to give?'"

"I know, just enjoy yourself," Lauren tells her.

"You'll know with time."

"The thing is," an excited Colette's says,

"I believe this guy, Jason English, is the guy. *My* guy. There's just something about him. Remember when I brought him to your attention at Tin Roof? I felt this way about him before we even met. When I looked at him from across the room, I felt it. And when he came over to me that night and introduced himself, our eyes locked. That's when I really knew."

There's something magical in the air and all three of them feel it. They look at each other as Pamela says,

"Okay Colette, are you putting your, 'in the vortex' vibe out right now? I know you are because we can all feel the energy."

"I feel it too," Lauren happily agrees with Pamela.

"It's warm, and hearing the events from last night makes me feel really good and safe."

"I'm telling you both I believe he *is* the one," Colette says.

"I know you feel it too."

Colette is so sure because she didn't feel this way when she met Alton, the love of her life. They met when she was 19 years old. They spent a summer together and realized they were soul mates. They were in love, but as fate would have it, they lived on opposite sides of the country. She on the West Coast and he, on the East. As time progressed, he moved on. Alton married and started a family. Colette never found anyone that piqued her interest or touched her heart like he did. Not until she met Jason. The difference she feels is — there is nothing immature about the way, she feels today. Infatuation is not in the equation. She has grown, and this is solid.

On that note, the three put their coffee cups on the designated shelf and walk out into this beautiful day toward Pamela's car. Once in the car they decide to take the coast and drive down Pacific Coast Highway to Fashion Island. On the ride down Colette poses a general question to both Pamela and Lauren.

"So, what have you been doing these past few days; anything to tell?"

Lauren is silent, which prompts Pamela to start with,

"What's up Lauren, cat got your tongue?"

Lauren's eyes get big, as if she's just been caught taking the last chocolate truffle. She the says,

"All right. I've seen Danny. He called and wanted to get together and talk, and I met him at Sea Legs for a glass of wine."

"How was that for you?" Colette asks with concern.

"You know Letty," Lauren begins,

"I'm not really sure. Danny is the love of my life, but right now, we're not on the same page in terms of our future. I want more than the party life and constant travel. Don't misunderstand me, I like that too, but I'm ready to begin a family. I want to feel secure."

"I can understand that Lauren." Pamela says.

"So, what are you thinking? What was he talking about?" Colette asks.

"He was saying that he misses me and it's hard to live without me. But I don't want to feel like I've coerced him into seriously committing." Lauren replies.

"Do you really believe Danny can be coerced into anything? Maybe your absence has made him realize he could actually lose you?" Pamela asks.

Colette chimes in,

"I think that's the case. Danny probably can't believe you really walked away from the relationship and began dating other guys. I know the two of you truly love each other, so what are your plans? Can you still see yourself spending your life with him?"

"Certainly. All I've wanted, since we met four years ago, is to spend all of my life with Danny." Lauren quickly responds.

The girls sit still for a few moments, before Lauren continues the discussion.

"If Danny shows me he's serious – get ready for a wedding, ladies."

Crepes Suzette

Ingredients
Crepes:
1 1/2 cups all-purpose flour
Pinch salt
3 eggs
1/2 cup sugar
2 cups milk
1 Tbsp. orange liqueur (recommended: Grand Marnier)
1 tsp vanilla extract
1 Tbsp. orange zest
1/2 cup clarified butter
Sauce:
1 1/2 cups freshly squeezed orange juice
2 Tbsp. sugar
2 tsp grated orange zest
2 Tbsp. orange liqueur (recommended: Grand Marnier)
3 oranges, peeled and sectioned
Vanilla ice cream, for serving
Source: foodnetwork.com

Eight

Manhattan Beach, January 2010, Suzette

Jason gets to his house and runs to the front door. Winded, he opens it and goes inside and heads directly to the laundry room and takes off his shoes and socks. After stepping out of his gear, Jason decides to go into his office. Naked, he walks over to his desk and writes the number he's gotten off the building of his potential restaurant. After jotting down a few additional notes Jason dials James' number. The cellphone rings a few times before James answers.

"Hey Jay."

"James, what you know good?" Jason asks.

"You and your return to the States, man" James says with excitement.

"What's up?"

"I want to schedule some time with you to get your architectural expertise. I need to hire you to design plans for my new venture." Jason says.

"This is exciting Jay. I take it France has prepared you to go for your dreams. Good for you man. When do you want to come into the office?" James asks.

"You got any space for me today?" Jason inquires.

"I certainly do," James answers.

"What about noon? It hasn't hit you yet, but I'm sure your body clock is off and jet-lag is going to pay you a visit around 3 or 4 o'clock today" James says.

"I believe you're right, but I am so excited I'd like to be productive before I hibernate until Wednesday," Jason says.

"Thank you, James. I'll be there at noon," Jason adds.

When the call ends, James pulls into his parking space at his company. He turns off the engine of his BMW and sits in the car. He remembers when they all talked about their dreams when they were at USC, the University of South Carolina. He was fascinated by design and architecture, David was drawn to the theater and vowed he'd become a respected actor. Jason – with his sinewy physique – always loved the intricacies of food. He marveled at the chemistry of cooking, just like the guy on The Food Network, Alton Brown. Jason was the best cook and said he was going to own his own restaurant.

Jason thinks back to that day at USC when they discussed their passions. He felt so proud of his friends, who are doing exactly what they said they would do. He smiles broadly and gives thanks to the universe that he was guided to that little space he knows is going to be the home of his first restaurant. Jason thinks it was divine intervention that he decided to take a run today and happened upon that little spot. He goes to his bathroom and turns on the shower. Standing under the warm running water, he continues to play back the days of college. As he continues to look back, the feeling that there's something missing from his life returns. Jason allows the thought to have its way and he begins to think that he wants to share his life with someone. He immediately considers Tin Roof and the wine tasting on Thursday night. He thinks, *Wouldn't it be amazing, if I were to meet my lady this week?*

James' Breitling watch lets him know Jason will be walking through the door to his office in a few seconds. And sure enough, the door opens. Jason stands there, tall, tanned and confident. Feeling certain that he is on the verge of having an incredible place for those who enjoy delicious food, beautiful wines and stimulating conversation. Certain about every aspect of his restaurant, Jason also feels some uncertainty because he has no idea what James is going to design for him; nor can he map out what's in store for his future. Yet, he's excited and ready to begin.

"Hey Jay, come on in and have a seat. Coffee or water – or are you in need of a stiff drink?"

The guys share a hearty laugh and Jason declines the latter and accepts coffee. James walks over to his bar and pours Jason a cup of wonderful Blue Mountain coffee, imported from Jamaica. Jason takes the cup from James.

"I really like your setup. I've got to let you know how proud I am of you. Before I arrived, I was reminiscing, remembering our dreams. Look at you. I have just walked into your dream, man." Jason says.

James is deeply touched by what Jason said and gives him a loving embrace.

"Thank you, Jay. You should know how proud I am of you. I was also thinking about all of us – me, you and Dave, and how we've manifested our dreams. I'm honored to be sharing this journey with you. Talk to me about your vision. What do you see when you walk into your restaurant? How is it laid out?"

Jason hands James the sketches he's drawn. His eye light up, as James is taking a look.

"Put voice behind these sketches," James tells him.

"I see round tables seating parties of four, six and eight. I hear laughter and I see new friendships being established. The place has got to have a nice sound system to accommodate the incredible music, which will help create the inviting feel of the restaurant. I hear the hostess say, 'Welcome to Neylan's,'" Jason says.

"I like that Jay," James says.

"When did you decide on the name?"

"I just did. I didn't have a clue initially," Jason responds.

"Is that a French name?" James asks.

"No, it's Turkish. It means 'Fulfilled Wish,'" Jason says.

"It just popped into my head when I was describing my place. What better name?"

James and Jason walk into an adjoining room and James heads to his drafting table. The friends then get to work. James takes Jason's ideas and creates wonderful sketches. He decides to design the restaurant with an eclectic and very comfortable feel. It will be full of open spaces, large windows that open out onto the ocean and various portions of the restaurant. The tables will be round, but designed by James, which means they will be spectacular. Each one different. Comfortable chairs with high backs. The acoustics will be phenomenal and the artwork – priceless.

Jason couldn't have designed it better. He is pleased his friend really knows him.

"I've got to make a call man before I can let you know when we can begin."

Jason stands up with the sketches in hand, and tells James he hopes to be back within a few weeks.

"But of course, I'll see you before that," he says.

The guys say goodbye and Jason gets in his SUV, and dials the number he copied this morning. The phone rings four times before someone answers.

"Hello?" The voice is clear and strong, yet very feminine.

Jason is a little nervous, and surprised someone actually answered.

"Hello. My name is Jason English. I'm looking for a space for my first restaurant and I literally ran across a building today with your number on it. Are you Suzette?"

There is silence, then the person says,

"Yes. I am Suzette."

"It's good to be speaking with you," Jason says with enthusiasm.

He's filled with joy that someone picked up the call.

"How did you find the number?" Suzette asks.

She sounds indifferent and continues,

"It was in an obscure place on a window."

Jason tells her of his run this morning and immediately requests a meeting.

"Can we meet to talk about the space? Is it still available for lease or for sale?" he asks.

He's sure he detects a French accent.

"Suzette," Jason says,

"can we schedule a day and time to meet this week?"

"Thursday at 2 p.m. MB Post." She quickly responds.

"I'll see you then, Suzette," Jason replies.

They end the call and Jason is relieved as he drives home. When he arrives at his place he pulls into the garage and hops out of the Rover with and extra spring in his step. He trots into his office with the tentative floor plans and reviews them again. He walks into his bedroom and changes from his slacks and shirt and puts on casual pants and a loose-fitting, soft T-shirt. Jason walks into the kitchen and looks in the refrigerator and sees nothing of interest. He suddenly finds himself really exhausted. He walks over to a pile of books in his office and selects one of the recipes. He plans to lay on the bed and read for awhile.

The Zen alarm clock chimes softly. Jason looks over at his nightstand. It's 11 on Wednesday morning. He lays there and thinks about the conversation he had with Suzette on Monday. *We meet tomorrow. That's exciting.* Jason decides to go to the athletic club. He grabs his gym gear and heads to the garage. He hops in the Rover and KPCC is on the radio. It's a great day!

When Jason arrives at the club he heads toward the locker room to put his bag away and get a basketball. He goes to one of the courts and begins to shoot free throws. He's in his element when he notices, someone scrutinizing him. She's interestingly pretty: Tall and slender, brown straight hair, green eyes and dark, olive skin. He dribbles the ball up to the woman watching.

"Do you play?" he asks.

Jason notices her hands. Her fingers are manicured; polish free, and slender like those of a pianist's. He's had an affinity for hands ever since he took piano lessons at 8 years old. Jason had a crush on his piano teacher, Ms. Movahill. He thought she was so pretty. The woman looks at him, yet doesn't answer. He reiterates.

"Do you – play ball?" Jason asks again.

"No – not anymore. I just admire those who do." She smiles and extends her hand.

"Bonjour. I am Suzette Blanchard."

Jason can't believe his ears. *Can this be her?*

"Do you have a building on the beach?" he asks.

Suzette looks at Jason playfully, through squinted eyes.

"Who's asking?" she says.

"I'm Jason English," he says.

He finishes with,

"*il me fait tres plaisir de vous rencontrer.*"

Suzette's eyes light up.

"*Etes-vous couramment?*" she asks.

Jason smiles broadly,

"Yes, I am," he says.

"How so?" She's curious.

"I'm Creole. My parents are from Louisiana, their parents are from France and Africa."

"Makes sense, *oui?*" he says.

"Ahh," Suzette sings.

"*Oui.*" She agrees.

Their hands are still interlocked.

"This is serendipitous. Meeting you like this," he says.

Their hands slowly relax and release. There's a spark igniting between them, yet Jason is a bit hesitant because this is the woman he is going to be doing business with. He doesn't want to mix business with romance.

"What are your plans later this afternoon?" Suzette asks, searching his face.

"I am flexible." Jason says.

Even though they'll be doing business together, he just couldn't resist what might be in store.

"Your thoughts?" he asks.

"I was thinking I could show you the building after our workouts. Are you up for that?" Suzette offers.

Jason doesn't hesitate and immediately replies,

"Yes. I'd love to see it."

He really does want to see the building, the sooner the better. He's excited to get Neylan's up and running. However, he's also very attracted to Suzette and is wondering just how to deal with this dilemma, of perhaps being her tenant if she doesn't sell him the building.

"I would like to spend at least two hours here, maybe three. I've only just arrived." Suzette says.

"Good. Sounds like a plan. Meet in the lobby at 3:30?" Jason says with a big smile.

"Three-thirty it will be," She says.

Suzette turns and walks toward the women's locker room. Jason dribbles the ball back inside the glass encasement of the court. *I can't believe it. Everything seems to be lining up for me.* He stands at the three-point line and, swoosh – nothing but net.

Suzette has had a pretty intense workout. She lifted weights, spent about an hour on the track, and did some stretches. *Je vraiment besoin de s'asseoir dans le jacuzzi.* She goes into the locker room and disrobes. Hops in the shower to rinse off and then goes to the jacuzzi. She steps in the warm water and closes her eyes. *It's been a long time since I've felt this excited about something. Even though I am not familiar with this man, it is nice to know I am able to get excited about someone other than Delice. What a nasty breakup. The timing could not have been worse.* Her eyes begin to tear up as she thinks to herself. *Grand-père* (grandfather) made his transition that following week. *Mon cœur a été brisé deux fois.* At least the person who found my number seems to be *facile à obtenir avec.* I know the breakup was for the best. Most things are. Suzette takes a deep breath and begins to quiet her mind. She allows her body to sink down in the water until it covers her neck. Her eyes remain closed while she simply relaxes.

Suzette is an active woman who appears to be much younger than her 40 years. Her body is toned and athletic, as she runs, plays tennis and rides horses. She carries a strong, yet subtle air of sensuality. She is non-pretentious and easygoing, bringing to mind a willowy tree, moving gracefully in the breeze. Usually she's pleasant and laid back. Anyone paying close attention can see what Suzette tries so hard to conceal. Nevertheless, her taunt, glowing skin, perfectly arched brows and *a way* about herself, gives it away every time. Her background is aristocratic. She's lived a very privileged life. Although she and Delice lived a *good* life together, it was not what she was accustomed to by any means. Delice was a professional man, but not of her caliber, and that never mattered to her. It all seems so fresh to her, like she just left Delice yesterday. *Mon grand-père.* What would be your guidance for me now?

It's 3:30 and Jason is standing near the entrance of the club, awaiting Suzette. She walks up and stands next to him. He looks over at her and smiles.

"You ready?" he asks.

"Yes, I am ready."

They go to their own cars and take off. When Jason sees the building, and walks over to it, he remembers that it was just a few days ago that he got home from Paris. Now he's standing in front of the first building he's considering for his restaurant. Jason is mindful of how nervous he is. He feels a little scared – then he feels silly for feeling that way. *Man. This might really happen.* Suzette approaches him and touches his arm. He looks at her. There is something there between them.

"Are you ready to see your first restaurant?" she asks.

There's a sincere smile on her face and in her eyes. She removes the keys from her jeans pocket and goes to open the door. Of course, the building is dusty, being that it is located on the beach. It is boarded up. Jason's wondering how dilapidated it will be on the inside and how much this may cost him. He's almost certain this is the place because the location is resonating with him: He's just trying to put things in perspective.

The key is inserted into the lock and the door opens easily. Suzette walks in first. Jason follows and is floored when he sees the space. It's larger than it looks from the outside. The walls are painted close to the colors he and James discussed. He can see his vision much more clearly. It is almost as if his dream is being rolled out in front of him. Suzette is watching Jason. She is pleased to possibly be able to be of service – that is if he decides the building works for him.

"So, *que pensez-vous?*" Suzette asks Jason.

A beaming Jason says,

"I think it's amazing! I couldn't have imagined it would actually look this close to what I have envisioned."

"Follow me, let's walk through the place." Suzettes says.

Jason is silent now and contemplative. The room is spacious with a bathroom on the east side. James will have to add another one on the other side. The ceilings have iron beams, which add some character. There are a few windows, but Jason knows he'll add huge floor-to-ceiling windows later. James has an idea that will be cost-effective and befit a restaurant on the beach. The flavor will be semi-upscale. Jason can't escape his joy. A smile invades his face. It is perfect for Neylan's.

"I love it," Jason tells Suzette.

They begin to laugh. Suzette laughs because she's relieved and Jason laughs because he's so happy and can't believe his good fortune.

"I was beginning to wonder if something had troubled you. You were so quiet," Suzette says to him.

"I am pleased that you are pleased with this place,"

Looking at her with concern, Jason says,

"May I ask you something?" She gives him the go ahead.

"The day I found your number, on the bottom over there in the window, it seemed as if you were hiding it. Like you didn't want anyone to see the number. There's not even a 'for sale' or lease sign on it. Is there a reason the number was in such an obscure place?" Jason asks, as he looks closely at her, sensing there is a story there.

"This building belongs to *mon grand-père* – well it did before he left us. He has since made his transition. *Je l'aimais tellement.*"

Suzette closes her eyes and inhales deeply, as if she can smell his scent. She is holding her hands over her heart. Opening her eyes, she says,

"We don't have to talk about this, but if you really want your question answered. …"

"Would you like to continue this conversation over a bite to eat and a glass of wine? I think that may be what you need to discuss this," Jason says.

"How thoughtful of you. I would love to." She says.

"I'll call Dominique's Kitchen; a nice little French restaurant in Redondo Beach. Unless it's changed in the year I've been away, it's quaint, easy dress code and has a great wine selection."

Jason is attempting to cheer her up. He senses her sadness.

"*Qui. Quelle benediction.*"

Her eyes begin to sparkle.

"Thank you. This is just what the doctor ordered."

"I know we're complete strangers, but we can take my car if you like?" Jason suggests.

"Are you sure? My truck is right there."

She points to a huge white, Ford Super Duty. Jason looks at her sweetly and smiles before he says,

"I'm sure."

He's thinking she looks to be too small for such a big truck. Suzette can feel what he's thinking because she knows what it looks like. She also knows what she's capable of handling, despite her looks. They begin to laugh out loud as if having read each other's minds, and they walk to over to the Rover. This will be one of their little jokes in the years to come. Jason walks to the passenger's side and opens her door. Suzette gets in and he closes it behind her. When he gets inside he turns off the radio, gets on his cell and calls the restaurant. After a brief conversation with the hostess, he lets Suzette know it's a go. Since it's a Wednesday evening, there's availability.

"It opens at 4 so we'll get there just in time to select any seat we want," says a playful Jason.

"You know what they say, *l'oiseau en avance attrape le vers.*"

They look at each other and smile.

They drive down Pacific Coast Highway toward Redondo Beach. Jason sees Dominique's and passes it to drive to the corner to avoid making an illegal U-turn. When they get to the small parking lot there are ample spaces. Once Jason parks the vehicle they have to wait a few more minutes before the restaurant opens its doors.

"This is such a good idea, Jason. Thank you. Talking about *mon grand-père* always causes me to become really emotional," Suzette says.

"Well of course it does. That's got to be hard – losing someone you loved so dearly," Jason says.

"I am so sorry for your loss."

"*Merci.* You know, the fact …,"

she pauses and corrects herself,

"that the building *was* his is one of the reasons I tried to hide my number. I wanted to keep him with me always."

Her eyes are now filled with tears. Jason is touched and he places his hand on top of hers. The door to Dominique's Kitchen opens. Jason reaches in the back of the SUV and finds a napkin and immediately hands it to Suzette. He hops out of the car and opens her door. She gets out of the SUV and Jason's hand is on the small of her back as he gently leads her toward the entrance.

The hostess is a petite young woman with velvety, dark chocolate skin. Her eyes are big and bright to match her beautiful, warm smile.

"Welcome to Dominique's Kitchen. You have the run of the house. No one's here but you. Sit anywhere you'd like," she says cheerfully.

"I'll follow you," she adds.

"Do you have a preference?" Jason asks Suzette.

"I'd like to sit there," Suzette says to Jason.

She shows the hostess as she walks over to a quaint table she spots in the corner of the main dining area. The hostess and Jason follow her. He pulls her chair out for her, and she gracefully sits down. The hostess places the napkin on her lap. Jason takes his seat and the hostess places a napkin on his lap. They thank her.

"Your waitress' name is Mica. She'll be right with you," the hostess says and walks away.

Mica approaches, tall, thin and blonde.

"Hi, welcome to Dominique's Kitchen. I'm Mica and I'll be serving you this evening." She hands them a menu.

"Can I start you off with a cocktail or a glass of wine?" she asks.

"I could really use a cocktail," Suzette says, emphasizing *really*.

"What would you like?" Jason asks.

"I'd like a martini. Chopin vodka – dirty – with three blue cheese-stuffed olives – straight up – shaken and extremely cold." Suzette is ready to unwind.

"And you, sir?" Mica asks Jason.

"I'll join her with the same but Hendricks gin instead of vodka," Jason says.

"Should I order a Crepes Suzette?" he says.

Jason's trying to lighten up her mood. She smiles and shakes her head no.

"I'll get those cocktails out for you. You can take your time and look at over the menus at your leisure," Mica says with a smiles and leaves.

"Two dirty martinis."

Mica says as she delivers the icy cold cocktails. She places two cocktail napkins in front of Jason and Suzette and sits the drinks on them.

"I'll come back and check on you once you've had time to enjoy your drinks and look over the menus. Would you like to hear the specials now, or shall I give you a moment?"

"I would like many moments," Suzette responds with a smile.

She looks over at Jason and smiles warmly.

"I believe we'll relax and enjoy these before we consider the specials," Jason says to Mica.

His and Suzette's eyes meet in agreement. Mica says,

"Of course," and smiles at them and walks away.

"*C'est parfait. Merci beaucoup. Un toast à vous* Jason." Suzette raises her glass to him.

She is extremely glad they've met and that he's going to own her late grandfather's building on the beach. *It's kismet.*

Jason raises his glass and responds.

"*Je suis d'accord. à votre santé.*"

They look at each other with a sense of comfort.

"It's cool to meet someone to speak French with," Jason tells Suzette.

"I know. It's really good," Suzette says, with a heavy accent.

"Are you ready to talk about what was bothering you earlier?" Jason asks.

His expression is compassionate and he reaches over and is once again touching her hand, offering comfort.

"Shortly before *mon grand-père* made his transition, I experienced an emotional breakup from Delice, my boyfriend for over 10 years. We were each other's everything. With time, it grew into something lovely. But then after additional time, it started to decline." She pauses.

"I guess we stopped paying attention to who we were becoming. We grew apart and finally gave up. Delice found a lover, and the knowledge of that – even though I knew we were through – *me déchira l'intérieur*. The split was surreal. Once I began getting accustomed to the void of not having Delice in my life, *mon grand-père* passed away. Since then I've come to the States to handle real estate business for my family. Such a fortunate break. It's been a blessing for me. I've been able to begin the healing process. And I must say I really appreciate meeting you." She finished with an exhausted "sigh."

She was'nt embarrassed by her honesty, nor was Jason.

"How are you healing? Is there a particular method you're following, or …" Jason's question drops off as Suzette begins to answer.

"I'm healing by reading spiritual books. *A Course In Miracles* to be exact, meditating, running and being inside myself. Thinking. The weather here is amazing and always cheerful. I know I am in the correct place." She looks over at Jason and then averts her eyes.

"Is there anything I can do?" he asks.

"I can't imagine what you've been going through. I am so sorry for your loss."

He squeezes her hand.

"Now it makes so much sense why the number was so difficult to find."

He looks at her thoughtfully and adds,

"Would it help if we run together some mornings? I'm an avid runner. It's like my music."

"Yes! That would be nice to have a running buddy while I'm here," she says with great joy.

She looks at her empty martini glass.

"I think food will be a good idea at this time," she says.

They are on the same page and Jason attracts Mica's attention. Mica reaches their table and asks,

"Are you ready to hear about the specials?"

They look at each other. They both have their eyes on the escargot, the roasted chicken and the Cesar salad.

"We've decided to keep it simple," Jason tells her.

He orders their meals and informs Mica they'll have a bottle of Conundrum with dinner and sparkling water for now. Mica acknowledges his request and heads toward the kitchen. Suzette sits quietly. She's enjoying being on a quasi-date. She's feeling good. Happy she's not at the house alone.

"So, Jason," Suzette begins,

"tell me, what is your story?"

Her accent is thicker now that she's had a cocktail. She looks at him, curiously. She has a natural, yet very soft air of sexuality about herself. Jason noticed this when they first met.

"What would you like to know, Suzette?" Jason says as he looks at her with interest.

"I live in Manhattan Beach. I've just returned from Paris, France, on Sunday. I lived there for one year attending culinary school, and I'm glad to be back." He says.

Jason really doesn't know where to go from here. He has become uncomfortable. He thinks she's beautiful and sexy. His thoughts go to her soft skin. He wonders how smooth her legs would be if he were to stroke them. He doesn't want to cross a line, which is where the discomfort is coming from. He tries to keep his composure.

"I'll be better at answering your questions if you ask them specifically."

That statement put him back in the driver's seat. He begins to relax and feel more like himself. Suzette didn't pick up on his thoughts. She had thoughts of her own.

"Did you leave someone behind when you went abroad to study?" she inquires.

Her tone is soft, yet serious. She's interested in him and not just as a potential business deal. Suzette is many things, but she's never afraid to go after what she wants. Jason fits the bill.

"No. Unfortunately, I came home to an empty house." He answers.

The thoughts Jason shared with his friends are heavy on his mind.

"I've been very focused for the past few years. Really no room for a relationship."

He looks intently at her, waiting for a response. Silence. When Suzette does speak, she looks confused.

"*Etes-vous* gay ? " Suzette looks disappointed.

"*Non, je l'ai vraiment été concentré et déterminé à avoir un grand restaurant. Je aime les femmes.* Just the thought of Suzette asking him if he was gay made him go into to full French. She began to apologized profusley.

"No. I've really been focused and determined to have a great restaurant. I love women."

Jason then realizes he's explaining so adamantly because he's quite interested in her. He gets a bit embarrassed and looks red in the face. She realizes he's blushing and smiles at him. She's relieved because at least she knows he's interested as well.

～

*S*uzette walks into the front door of a beautiful house on the Strand. She tosses her keys into a huge bowl of blown glass. Before her is a large living room decorated with white modern furniture, peppered with bright colored pillows. Large, tasteful pieces of original art made by California artists dress the walls. The house has hardwood floors partially covered by a large Moroccan area rug. There are huge windows to let in the natural light and the ocean views. The house is approximately 5,000 square feet with panoramic views of the ocean. She walks into an office, past the living room and plops down in front of a television-sized computer screen. She goes directly to the property on the beach. Once she pulls up the photograph of the building and the paperwork, she presses save and walks into the kitchen. Going to the wine glasses as if on automatic pilot, then to the refrigerator, she pours her favorite white wine, walks out onto her patio and takes in the beautiful ocean air. She's happy it's only 7:45. She can sit on the patio chaise lounge and think. *Jason English. I like him.* Her mind goes from Jason to her grandfather, and then it ends up on Delice. She just can't get him out of her mind and that frustrates her. *I'm not ready. Bon sang!* He is charming and kind and she really likes him but … *I'm just not ready yet. Personne ne dit amour était juste.*

Suzette is wise enough to know that if Delice can enter her mind on the same thread Jason is occupying, then that means something. She would rather not include anyone else in any drama or confusion she may be experiencing. That is just not the thing to do. She is certain her grandfather would love Jason if he were around to meet him. The thought of her *grand-père* makes her smile. Suzette's cellphone rings and she can tell by the number it is her close friend from Paris. She smiles, answers the call, and begins to speak French

Feta Cheese Pizza

1 large crust/ homemade or pre-made
4 large Roma tomatoes
As many garlic clove slices as you like
Olive oil
½ Tbsp. sugar
½ bunch torn basil
1 pack of feta cheese

Nine

*C*ollette's car pulled up in front of Jason's house. She was dressed casually and ready to spend the day with him. Before she could exit the car, he was out on the sidewalk to greet her. He motioned for her to park on the right side in his driveway. Colette had butterflies in her stomach – you know the kind that come to visit when you first meet someone you like. The little flirty ones that just seem to want to flutter and flip all through your belly. Colette was excited, and believe it or not she welcomed the feeling, as it indicated to her that she was really close to love; and what a divine place to be.

When she reached for her door handle to get out of the car, Jason was opening it for her. He took her hand and helped her out. They stood there like two little children, beaming through the light of their smiles. They were almost laughing until Jason started talking.

"You know I would have preferred to come to your home and pick you up. It really wouldn't have mattered to me."

He was very sincere as he looked at Colette.

"I know Jason, but you're closer to Malibu than I, and it just makes sense that I come to you."

She was looking back at him, and it was easy to share a direct gaze. Jason smiled at Colette and took her hand, leading her through the garage, since that door was up.

"Come in and have a glass of water of something. I have organic tea. Which would you like?" he asked.

"I'm good, thank you Jason."

She looked around the room.

"Your house is nice," She said,

"Oh," he said as though he had forgotten his manners.

"Let me give you a tour."

Again, he took her hand and walked her through each room of the house. He showed her his nice backyard with a pool and a cozy patio area. They slowly walked back into the house through the back door.

"Are you ready to go to the Getty?" Jason asked.

She said she was and they got in his Rover and headed north. Once on the 405 Freeway the two felt pretty easy with each other. Colette crossed her legs on the seat in the lotus position and Jason's hand found its way to the fold of her leg, where the calf and the thigh meet. Everything was easy. They rode along in silence and familiarity when Jason broke the silence.

"I'm going to host a taste test in a few weeks," He said.

He wanted to bounce his ideas off her to hear her thoughts on it. For some reason, he felt she'd have significant input. Colette took a moment to consider his words. *A taste test.*

"I think that's a great idea. Do you know who you might invite?" she responded.

Colette was curious, and she began thinking of ways she could help him. …

The couple never made it to the Getty. They wanted to get into each other's heads and decided to go to West L.A. to the farmers market on Fairfax. They were both into it.

Sandwich

2 thick slices of crusty artisan bread
Roast turkey slices
Cranberry relish or jam of your choice
Thick slices of brie cheese
Heat sandwich to melt the brie and serve

Ten

*T*he girls decide to split a sandwich and a salad. They beckon Betty-Mae, who is prompt and pleasant.

"Y'all ready to order?" she asks.

"Yes," Colette says with a smile.

"We're thinking about sharing a sandwich and a salad. What do you think, Betty-Mae, the Brie or Crab sandwich?"

"I enjoy them both," Betty-Mae said.

"But since your friend's never been here before I'd go with the Brie sandwich and a simple field of greens salad."

"Perfect, well that's what we'll have," Colette says.

"Sure you don't want truffle fries to start?" Betty-Mae asks.

"After all, you are celebrating."

The girls are tempted, but stay with the salad choice. Karen looks at Colette and asks,

"How do you handle it when you and Jason have an argument? Do you find that you argue more or less now that you are married?"

"We really aren't the people who argue much. When we met we were basically in sync, across the board. At times, we may feel a brief disconnect, but I believe that's because Jason shuts down when he's experiencing stress of any kind. He's from the old school in terms of protecting his wife. He doesn't like me to worry about anything, but he fails to realize his inability or unwillingness to communicate with me isn't good for me. Other than that, we're always good," Colette says.

"I wouldn't worry about that, the arguing thing. I've found that things are usually what they were before you were married. There's just more security, and that goes for both of you. You both feel as though you can breathe; and by that, I mean being yourself is not a deal breaker." Colette says.

"I like that. David and I are good. He is really, as I've said before, a stand-up guy. I'll just be certain to keep my eyes open for the shut down," Karen says.

They both laugh and the food arrives. The sandwich is evenly divided into two portions on two plates accompanied by the salad. They order another bottle of champagne and continue lunch. Late into the lunch, Betty-Mae comes by and says,

"If it's not being unprofessional, I'd like to say, I think it's nice you ladies are taking the time to celebrate the coming marriage."

Both Colette and Karen smile and let her know her comment is welcomed.

When they finished their meal, Betty-Mae pours the last of the champagne into their flutes and clears their table. For a while the two ladies are quiet, then as if occupying the same mind, they say in unison,

"Let's go back to Carol Saunders and look at wedding rings!"

Giggles of delight ensue and they lift their glasses. They quickly finish their libations and beckon for Betty-Mae. When she arrives at their table she presents them with an individual- sized flourless chocolate cake, accompanied by two forks.

"Since you ladies were so good during lunch, I just couldn't help bringin' you my favorite dessert. I figured what woman doesn't like chocolate, and besides, somebody's getting married!"

All the women begin to laugh.

"My treat," Betty-Mae says.

"Well how can we say no to that?" Karen says.

Each of them pick up their fork. Betty-Mae slips away and the two friends indulge in the rich, decadent, delectable treat. When Betty-Mae brings their check, she tells them of the pleasure she's had serving them, wishes Karen good luck and walks away.

"This is my treat" Colette says to Karen.

She pays the bill, leaving Betty-Mae a hefty tip. Karen thanks Colette and with much excitement, they make their way back to Carol Saunders.

When the two walk back into the store, Karen heads across the room to the same counter she was viewing when Colette greeted her before lunch earlier that day. There is a ring she has her eye on and she scans the inventory for it.

Ah, there it is, she thinks. Karen then looks for someone to help her. She spots a lovely, middle-aged woman standing at the other end of the counter. The woman looks up as if Karen has called her name. She walks over to Karen and smiles.

"I believe something's caught your eye," she says with a sexy, Southern drawl.

"I'll show it to you if you point it out to me."

Karen's eyes are bright as she points to a ring.

"That one. I'd like to see that one." Karen says.

The woman takes the key she's wearing around her wrist and unlocks the back of counter that is housing the ring, and gently takes it off a stand. As she lays the ring down on the red velvet cushion on the counter, she says,

"Isn't this a beautiful ring. What's the occasion; wedding or anniversary?"

"I'm getting married. My boyfriend has asked me to marry him and to look at rings. I like this one," she says as she places the canary yellow diamond ring on her finger.

"The yellow is such a beautiful contrast against your dark skin," the jeweler compliments.

Karen looks at the ring and agrees with her. She looks at her hands and thinks she has nice hands. Karen begins to think about Dave and what a wonderful man he is, as Colette walks up and puts her hand on top of hers. She looks at the ring, saying,

"That is beautiful! It's so perfect against your skin."

"I know," Karen says.

"You know," Karen continues,

"I'm just looking to see what I like. Dave asked me to look at rings while he is away and then we can go shopping and pick one together."

"That is so romantic," Colette says.

Karen continues to admire the ring on her finger.

---

s Karen unlocks the door to her spacious home in Heathwood, she realizes she didn't buy anything. Karen's shopping spree leaves her empty-handed. *I have more than enough clothes and shoes. I don't need or want for anything. My ring and my wonderful man are all that concern me.*

Karen is happy and smiles when the phone rings, with David on the other end.

"Hi Baby," Karen says as she smiles broadly.

"How's it going out there?"

David informs her he has been selected out of 10 others to play the principal role in a new movie produced by a former female producer of a very successful show.

"What does that mean Baby? Are you coming home as planned or are we moving back to L.A.?" she inquires.

David tells her he'll be home tomorrow.

"Tomorrow?" Karen answers, surprised since David has not been gone long.

"I'd like to go ring shopping if you don't have any other plans," he says.

"Of course, David. I'd love to go and shop for rings. It's interesting you should say that, because Colette and I were in Carol Saunders jewelry store today,"

"And?" David asks.

"And I looked at rings, David. I saw a beautiful canary yellow diamond ring. …"

And before she could finish her sentence, David says,

"Looked beautiful on your dark skin."

"Yes, David! It was gorgeous! I loved it. Hurry home and I'll show you the ring. But I really want to hear about your lead role."

Karen tries to muffle her enthusiasm about her ring as David's huge career-changing news is far more important.

"This is a new thing for you; the lead role in a movie. We've got to celebrate. May I tell Colette and Jason?"

David's excited and proud as he shares the good news. He's thinking that Karen never has to work again unless she wants to, since he has been smart with his money, and now this will be the tip into real financial security that he needs.

"Yes, my beautiful bride-to-be. You may tell Colette and Jason." he says.

"This is so surreal David. You never even go for the lead role of any movie. How did this happen?" Karen is excited.

David responds,

"I never wanted to battle with anything that has to do with what I really enjoy doing and can make a living at. But the story gets more interesting. This part was written for me. The producer has been a fan of my work. Can you believe that? I'm just really happy that I've been given this opportunity."

On the way home Colette stops by Montshoh's, their second restaurant, the first one is Neylan in Manhattan Beach. She walks into the kitchen and Jason's not there. That's because he's in the dining area talking to customers. That's his favorite thing to do. She peeks out and sees him smiling and talking to a new couple. He acts as if they've been friends forever. That's one of the reasons his restaurants are so successful. As Jason turns to walk to another table he sees his best friend peeking at him. He smiles at her. Colette winks at Jason and he proceeds to the other table. She thinks of how sexy her husband is and how he still does "that thing" to her. Standing there deep in brief thought, Jason walks through the doors and grabs her.

"Hey Beautiful," he says with genuine enthusiasm.

"You still take my breath away," Colette says. She smiles at Jason as she looks deep into his eyes. He returns the gaze and quickly steals a kiss before saying,

"I'll be home soon Lety."

"See you later," Colette says, and walks out the back door. Getting into her car she thinks of Jason and how far they've come in such a short amount of time. She remembers meeting him and how it now seems to have occurred only yesterday. *My, how quickly the days become years.* With a great smile on her face and deep love and appreciation in her heart, her cellphone rings. Colette pushes her answer call button,

"Hey there little miss bride to be. You okay?"

"Where are you? Do you have a minute to pop by?" Karen asks with excitement.

"Well of course I have a moment to stop over. Jason's still at Montshoh's, and will probably be home in a couple of hours. Are you okay?" Colette inquires.

"Yes I am. Just get over here," Karen says.

With that, Karen ended the call. Colette heads in the direction of Heathwood. She pulls into the driveway in front of the garage door. She gets out of the car and walks up the sidewalk that leads to David and Karen's front entrance. The house is a nice Tudor home. The front door is classic, and before Colette could ring the doorbell, the door opens. Karen stands in front of her about to burst.

"Come in and have a seat. I know we've been celebrating all day, but do you have any room to do just a bit more of that?" Karen asks with a tone of, *please do.*

"Any time a friend of mine wants to celebrate I'm all in," Colette tells her.

She follows Karen into the den and sits on a bar stool. Karen is going toward the refrigerator and takes out a bottle of champagne. Colette gives Karen a mischievous look.

"Well I know you're not pregnant since we're going to be partaking yet again in a delicious libation," Colette says.

Karen begins to laugh and pours the bubbly into each flute. Then she tells her,

"David has been given a huge opportunity! He's landed the lead role in a movie that is being produced by one of our favorite females in the business. And the thing is, he didn't even audition for it. David never goes for the lead. But listen to this. They wrote the part for him!"

Colette is following her every word. When Karen is finished,

"That's incredible news! They wrote a part specifically for him. So, what's next? Does this wonderful news mean you'll be moving back to L.A.?" Colette asks.

The girls sit in silence for a brief second.

"I don't know," Karen finally replies.

"I didn't ask him because he was so excited. He'll be home tomorrow. ..."

"Tomorrow?" Colette asks with surprise.

"I know L.A. is only a plane ride away, but wasn't he going for … just his regular type role?" Colette asks.

"Yes," Karen concurs.

"We thought he was hired to play his usual role of a nondescript guy, which we also believed no one really pays attention to. That's all I know so … let us toast, yet again!"

The two sit in the den at the bar and sip champagne and have small talk about the things they like to talk about.

Later, when Colette pulls into her garage she doesn't see Jason's car and she's glad she beat him home. She grabs her bags, because unlike Karen she wasn't ring shopping, and dashes into the house. Colette hangs her new garments and jumps in the shower. She lets the water run over her body and she stands there thinking about what she and Karen just talked about. *Things can change as quickly as the blink of an eye. Nothing is ever etched in stone, that's for sure. We just never know.* As she applies her shower gel, her thoughts shift to Jason and how much she loves him. One of her purchases was a simple, silk, eggshell white, billowy lounging outfit. After drying off and putting on lotion, Colette slips it on and falls on the bed. In song she says,

"I feel so beautiful. This is so nice."

In the kitchen now, Colette decides to create a little appetizer plate for her and Jason. She pulls out a few cheeses, some olives and a few mini tomatoes. She then cuts some crusty bread and gets the pate and places a small knife on the platter near it. She walks into the dining area and places the platter and two cocktail plates on the table. She sets the ambiance to feel romantic, dimming the lights, lighting a few candles, and putting on Alpha. She finally sits down and relaxes. She's drinking a sparkling water waiting for Jason. After about 20 minutes he walks into the house.

"Hey, Gorgeous!" Jason says.

"Hey Lover-Man," Colette responds.

Jason walks in and smiles broadly noticing the candles. He walks over to Colette, bends down and kisses her. His eyes are bright.

"I'm glad you're home," she says with a huge smile.

"I'm glad I'm home too." Jason says, kissing Colette again.

He then sits down across from her and she pours a glass of red wine for them both. She raises her glass.

"This toast is to David. May his lead role bring him many more," she says.

She looks at Jason smiling as if she's let the cat out of the bag. Jason lifts his glass as well and responds to Colette's toast.

"And may we all have a great time at the Academy Awards!"

"Jason!" Colette says laughingly.

"How did you know?"

"David called and told me after he was informed the role was created specifically for him. He was dazed because it came as such a surprise."

"Oh," Colette says, sounding as if she's whispering the word.

Jason leans across the table and gives Colette a sweet kiss on the nose. She gazes up at him as if she's thinking about something.

"I love you," she says.

"I like it when you wait up for me, Letty," Jason became serious.

"You know how involved I get with the customers," he says.

"I know," Colette responds,

"and besides the delicious food prepared there, *you* are the reason your customers so enjoy Montshoh's. It's always fine when you're there having a nice time with your peeps. I think it's wonderful. You understand that your kindness and sweet spirt is what made me fall in love with you, don't you?" She looks sweetly at him and smiles warmly.

"I know baby. Thank you for that," Jason responds.

He stands up.

"Let's go sit in the living room. Would you like that?" he suggests.

She nods her head and walks with Jason to the living room. Once they cozy up on the couch Colette looks at Jason and lets out a sweet sigh.

"Baby, I've been trying to decide on the best time to bring this up. I'm not sure, of what's been going on with you lately," she says.

Jason respectfully listens to her.

"I've been feeling you pull away – or should I say shutting down," Colette says.

"Oh Letty, sweetheart," Jason says.

"I'm here. I'm for you and I'm so sorry to have put you through this. I've been trying to find the best opportunity to talk to you about this."

Colette begins to worry.

"Whatever it is Jason, you know we've got this," Colette assures him.

I love this woman so much. Jason thinks as he takes Colette's hand.

2010 – Manhattan Beach

When Jason pulls into his garage he's feeling energetic. The effects of the cocktail and wine have since faded, and he's excited about the day. To have met Suzette was serendipitous. It was great on two fronts. She is sexy and quite interesting, and she may be the person who sales him the home of his first baby, Neylan's. Once he gets inside he goes directly into his office and dials James' number. He puts the call on speaker and goes over to the drafting table and begins looking at the plans he and James created on Monday. After the third ring James answers the call.

"Hey Jay!" he says enthusiastically.

"What do you know good?"

"Hey man." Jason's tone is a-matter-of-fact.

"I'll tell you what I know if you're ready for it." He pauses.

"I met the woman behind the hidden number on the building that so intrigued me," Jason says.

"You've got to be kidding me! How did that happen?" James says with surprise.

"Weren't you supposed to meet her tomorrow?" James asks.

James is curious, but there's a little chuckle behind his question. He's aware of how the women see Jason. Jason is – after all – a tall, successful and very handsome, charming man – who is also a really good guy.

"How'd you pull that one off?" James inquires.

"I didn't pull anything off," Jason says, jokingly coming to his own defense.

"And yes, I was scheduled to meet her tomorrow, but I was at the club today and this woman was watching me shoot hoops. I went over to introduce myself and it was her. Suzette."

Jason tells the story with fresh surprise, still not really believing his good fortune.

"We ended up having an early dinner at Dominique's Kitchen." Jason says, as if he has *je ne sais quoi.*

"Leave it to you to bump into the owner of your potential new business spot. And, oh yeah, she is a woman. So?" James teases.

"What was the deal? Anything to speak of? Any sparks?" James really wants to know.

"Yes man, there was an attraction. She's sexy, interestingly beautiful, adventurous, and she's French. You know I love that, but I'm hesitant to take it any further at this stage of the game," Jason explains.

"We may be doing business together and I don't want to blur the lines. If anything is meant to be, it will happen."

"There you go with your philosophical reasoning. I thought you wanted 'your woman,' man. At least you can get laid." James can't help but be himself.

There was a brief silence before they both began to laugh.

"I knew you were thinking that, but you know there's more to me than that. Don't think the idea didn't cross my mind. But remember, there's always more to the story," Jason says.

James shakes his head in agreement on the opposite end of the call.

"So, what's up?" James asks.

"I just got home and pulled out what we did on Monday. You think you want to come by and go over some things?" Jason asks.

"I feel really good about this. I was able to do a walk-through of the building." Jason is excited.

"Certainly man. I'll be here for another hour or so. You got any Chopin over there?" James inquires.

"You know I do. See you when you get here," Jason says as they end the call.

The doorbell rings at around 9 and Jason opens it to James and David. The two, walk in. They're both excited for him.

"Now you know I couldn't be left out of the loop regarding something as important as this!" David says.

The friends embrace.

"Dave, you know this is how we do it," Jason says with bright eyes.

"Jay, have you changed anything since you've returned?" James says as he heads to the bar.

"No, it's still the same. I've been back for three days James." Jason is pleased they are together.

"The Chopin, tonic, vermouth, olives, ice and glasses are all in the same place. You know how to help yourself," Jason says.

James is already there, making himself a martini.

"Does anybody else want one?" James asks.

"Make mine a gin and tonic with lime," David says.

"I'll have what you're having," says Jason.

"Got it fellas. I'll bring them into the office," James says as the others head in that direction.

It's a Wednesday night at 9 and the guys are together again. It seems as though they've never missed a beat. The energy is high. This is a project they are all working on. Since David's acting career is pretty solid and James' company is doing well, they want to help bring Jason's dream to fruition. James brings the drinks in and Jason offers a toast.

"In gratitude."

The others repeat the toast and their glasses meet.

"Let's get this show on the road," James says.

Jason gestures toward the drafting board.

"But first, may we please have a word about the lovely lady who owns this building?" David insists playfully.

"I'd love to hear about her, because I'd really like to know how you can only be home for three days and meet this woman. Who, by the way, I understand shared sparks with you," David says. The guys were giving Jason a hard-time, and, and Jason began to feel enthused. He tells his friends about the encounter with Suzette and how there was definitely chemistry between them. Jason told them of his decision to hold off on anything romantic until the business was handled. The guys agreed, telling Jason he was certainly making the right decision. But it had to be James to say,

"Well there's still tomorrow night at Tin Roof. You never know what you may find when you least expect it."

Jason agrees, yet thinks more about Suzette. There was a little something between them. He could see himself with her – well at least from the little he's seen. He'll go to Tin Roof, but he's not thinking about meeting anyone. How often does that happen? He lived in Paris, the city of love, for a year and is still single. …

⌒

Colette is still looking at Jason. Something about all of this is making her want to cry. She begins to feel sad and feels like she could be sick. Still looking directly, yet curiously at him, Jason's expression and body language conjures up feelings in Colette she's not felt in a long time. A lone tear escapes her eye and finds its way down her cheek. She looks at him, and never expecting anything like this, her words surprise even her.

"Jason – is someone else involved in this – your inconsistent emotions?" Colette askes.

She can feel something is up. She knows she's right. Her body never lies. Jason is involved with another woman. Colette slowly withdraws her hand from his and feels the blood drain from her body. She's not really, sure how to feel, because she doesn't feel infidelity is the problem. She's confused.

"Who's this person, Jason?"

Jason is in a state of temporary freeze. He can't speak.

"How long Jason?" Colette continues.

She's not interested in guilt games or manipulation. She just wants to know the story. This is so surreal to her.

⟜

*J*ason feels horrible. He doesn't want this to be happening right now. He wonders why he's messed this up. *Nothing even happened! Why was I keeping it a secret?*

Roasted Whole Chicken

Ingredients

- 1 2-lb. whole roasting chicken, innards removed
- 1 lemon, halved
- 2 cloves garlic, whole
- 2 stems fresh rosemary
- 4 sage leaves
- 2 Tbsp. olive oil
- Salt and pepper to taste

Instructions

1. Preheat oven to 450 degrees.
2. Fill the cavity of the chicken with the lemon, sage, rosemary and garlic. Rub the outside of the chicken with the olive oil and season it liberally with salt and pepper.
3. Place in preheated oven and roast for about 10 minutes. Lower oven temperature to 350 degrees and continue roasting until a thermometer placed in the dark meat (thigh) reads 155 degrees.
4. Remove from oven and let the chicken rest for 10 minutes or until the internal temperature rises to 165 degrees.
5. Carve chicken and serve with the roasted lemon and fresh herbs. Great served with a glass of Italian red wine

Eleven

HUNTINGTON BEACH, 2010
THE FIRST TIME

*J*ason remembers when he and Colette became serious. He had called to invite her out for dinner in Santa Monica. She'd mentioned never having eaten at Melisse, an excellent French restaurant offering a true fine dining experience and, one of the most expensive restaurants in the country. He wanted to introduce her to such an experience, but when they spoke, Colette asked him if she could take a rain check. She wanted to treat him this time by preparing dinner. Jason was touched by Colette's sweet invitation. He graciously accepted.

That Friday evening Jason arrived at Colette's promptly at 6:30. He brought beautiful large, white tulips and two bottles of the finest wines from France; one white and the other Burgundy. The ambiance was romantic, with candle light throughout and fresh flowers. Regina Carter's *Cinema Paradiso* filled the air. Jason breathed in the sound of the violin as he handed Colette the bouquet. He leaned in and gave her a gentle peck on the lips.

"You look beautiful," Jason said, looking at Colette with twinkling eyes.

She was wearing a simple, loose-fitting beaded cotton mini dress by Aofuli.

"Thank you, Jason," says Colette, holding the flowers in her hand with a big smile.

"I'm going to put these in some water. Make yourself at home."

Colette went out of the room to retrieve a vase. Jason headed for the kitchen to relieve himself of the wine he was holding. Something smelled delicious and he wondered what it was.

"Colette!" Jason projected.

"It smells really good in here. May I ask what you are preparing?"

He looked around the kitchen and felt comfortable in her house. Colette walked in and stood behind him as he surveyed the kitchen as most chefs would do.

"Yes you may, Mr. English," she said sweetly.

She felt relaxed around him and liked him being in her kitchen looking at everything, seeing who she is. Colette was glad she'd decided to have Jason over for dinner. He's such a kind and generous man – she wanted to do something really special for him.

"I'm preparing a whole chicken with rosemary, sage and garlic, and a field of greens salad," she said.

"That sounds like something I can't wait to eat. The wines I brought over will pair well with your meal, unless you have others in mind," Jason says.

"No, the wines you've brought are great. Would you like to open a bottle now?" Colette asked.

"*Absolument.* Where is your corkscrew?" Jason asked, folding a little French into his response.

Colette left it up to him and he decided they'd have the red before dinner. While Jason opened the wine Colette brought two glasses over to him. He poured the wine and they walked into the living room. Colette sat on a chair and Jason on the couch. They were both unsure of how to navigate themselves in this space together. Usually they were out or they'd just pop into the other's home for a brief moment. Tonight, they would be spending time together, alone at Colette's house.

After their first glass of wine Jason mustered up the courage to ask Colette to come sit on the couch near him.

"Colette, would you mind coming a little closer? I feel you are too far from me."

Colette blushed at the question. She walked over to the couch and Jason extended his hand toward hers. She took his hand and he guided her to sit close enough that their legs touched. Colette felt nervous. Her stomach had butterflies and she was reminded of having a high school crush. Jason kept her hand in his. His thumb slowly traced each knuckle and each crevice of her fingers. He looked directly into her eyes.

"Your glass is empty," Jason said to her, almost in a whisper.

"I'd like to refill it."

Colette seemed to be in a slight trance when she responded.

"I'd like you to, Jason. That'd be nice."

Their eyes were locked. She was relaxed. Jason reached over and got the wine bottle. He poured for Colette and then for himself and she took a sip of the wine, looking at his hand on hers. She loved his large hands and how they seemed so protective. Jason watched Colette as she watched him continue to trace her hands with his thumb, never letting go. First over each knuckle – down each finger – then to the palm of her hand, tracing her lifeline and on to her wrist. Colette was almost breathless. Jason kept his gaze on her as he took her glass from her hand and sipped the wine. He placed it on the coffee table and gently pulled her close.

"Colette," Jason said, his voice was low and wanting.

"I'm going to kiss you right now, and I don't know where that may lead. Do I have your permission?"

His body felt warm and excited, nervous with anticipation for her. Getting ahead of himself, visualizing what this encounter was going to be, Jason was also imagining his and Colette's lives together.

"Yes." Colette responded in a breathless whisper.

She too, was full of anticipation. As Jason began kissing her, his hand remained on hers and began to travel up her arm, lightly stroking and caressing it. His touch felt like feathers, which sent a message directly to the part of her that wanted to be explored by him. She could feel his hands on her. He discontinued the kiss and stood up, took Colette's hand again, only this time he asked her to show him the way to her bedroom.

⌒

*J*ason stood in the entrance to the bedroom as Colette walked through. She turned to look at him.

"Stand there, near the end of the bed." Jason directed.

His voice was deep and instructive. Colette walked over and stood near the end of the bed. The wheels in her head were turning, her heart was pounding. *What does he have in mind?*

"Step out of your shoes and lie on your back on the bed," Jason told her.

Colette did as she was told. Jason continued to stand at the door, looking at her. His eyes were sexy and she felt his yearning for her. As if teasing Colette, Jason took his time getting there. With each step he announced a clue of what he was going to do to her. She felt like she was going to explode, she was so excited and she so wanted this to happen. *How long have I been waiting for this? For Jason English?* Nevertheless, Colette restrained herself from any movement. When she could no longer tolerate his seduction, Jason was beside her, sitting on the bed. Placing his large, warm hand on her thigh, he leaned over, ever so closely to her ear, and simultaneously slid his hand higher, as he whispered,

"Listen to my breathing."

With that, Colette lost it, she sighed and her body squirmed rhythmically. Jason traced her clothed body with his hands. This time his touch was firmer than before. Colette listened to his breath as he inhaled and exhaled. Sometimes a small groan would escape him, which excited her. Colette's mini dress had shifted up, exposing her white silk panties. She wanted Jason to touch her there. He did not. Instead, he began breathing hot, moist air on her neck and ear, while rubbing her all over.

"Turn over. I want to see you from the back," Jason instructed.

Colette was really turned on by this. She wanted more instructions, more commands of things he wanted her to do. She laid on her stomach. Jason cupped her butt in his hands and then began appreciating her beautiful legs. He went directly to the back of her knees with warm breath and gentle kisses. Colette thought she'd faint from the excitement when finally, she felt Jason's hand on her – there. She let out a loud moan and Jason gently turned her on her back. He mounted her.

"Look at me. I want to see you."

Colette opened her eyes.

*Jason had just seen the building of his new restaurant the day before, now he and James were spending a lot of time on the plans and the building. Suzette went back to France a few days after she and Jason met. She and Jason had a huge attraction, yet were never able to consummate the emotions. They remained in touch – but it wasn't really a long-distance relationship. They both knew better than to play that game. Jason had fallen in love with Colette and Suzette was dealing with her personal angst in Paris.

The evening after she and Jason met, Suzette realized she was still carrying feelings for Delice. The next morning when they went running she informed him that she would be leaving for Paris on Monday to handle unfinished business. Jason was disappointed and a bit relieved, as he didn't want to confuse things between them. But with Jason's luck, he met Colette at the wine tasting at Tin Roof, the night Suzette said she was leaving. The two of them enjoyed a farewell dinner at the Strand House that Saturday night. Jason wouldn't see Suzette again until she appeared at Neylan's grand-opening party.

Caramelized Onion Tart with Gorgonzola and Brie Cheese

Ingredients

2 Tbsp. olive oil
4 cups of <u>sliced onions, sliced root-to-top into 1/4-inch thick slices</u>
(about 2-3 med. onions)
1 Tbsp. brown sugar
2 Tbsp. balsamic vinegar
1/2 tsp salt
1/2 tsp pepper
8 oz frozen puff pastry (defrosted a couple hours in the fridge)
2 oz chilled Brie cheese, rind removed and diced
2 oz Gorgonzola or other blue cheese, diced
2 Tbsp. chopped fresh tarragon

Twelve

eylan's. I like that name. I've never asked Jason where he came up with that one. I'm going to remember to ask him tonight. Colette made certain she had purchased a lovely cream-colored, Haute Hippie sheath dress, cream and bronze Manolo Blahnik shoes and a tiny Chanel bag. She was supper excited for him, tonight was his grand-opening party. He'd invited the who's who from California to New York City. Foodies from all over would be there. When they talked about it last night, he seemed so composed. As she continued to dress, she yelled into to the living area of the house to make sure Pamela and Lauren were not getting impatient.

They couldn't believe Colette's good fortune. One minute they were all going to Manhattan Beach to a wine tasting and a look-see, and the next thing they know – Colette is in love and her new beau is opening a restaurant. She walked out of her dressing room and they all headed to the car in the garage. On the drive to the South Bay, Pamela asks Lauren about Danny. Everyone in the car is curious. Lauren tells them *that* is on hold at the moment, and requests to change the subject. Something must be up.

When they arrive at Neylan's, the valet takes Colette's keys. The three enter the restaurant. There are those little lights everywhere, just like she likes them. The *Girl From Ipanema*, by Joao Gilberto and Stan Getz, fills the air. The restaurant is packed. The feeling is cozy, despite the fact that it's not a small place. James certainly has a way about capturing the ambiance of his client's visions. Colette and her girlfriends all think Neylan's is lovely and romantic.

"I feel like I'm at a spectacular Christmas party!" Colette told her friends.

As the three ladies took in their surroundings, Jason approached them. A waitress is next to him carrying a bottle of Krug 1998 Clos du Mesnil Chardonnay champagne, with three flutes. She poured the ladies a glass as Jason and Colette embraced and shared a tasteful kiss.

"Welcome to Neylan's ladies," Jason says as he takes Colette's hand.

"Would you excuse us for a brief moment?" he says to Pamela and Lauren.

The two of them walk over to a cabana. As they seem to stroll away from the girls, Jason asks Colette what she thinks of the finished building and the turnout.

"I love this place! I think you and James have done an incredible job! And Jason … the turnout couldn't have been more successful. Your public relations firm hit it out of the park. I'm sure your backers are really impressed." Colette says.

She looks in Jason's eyes and he kisses her. The moment is sweet. After their special moment, Jason thinks he should go out and mingle with all of his guests, and he makes Colette aware of it.

"I'll go and find the girls," she says.

Before they leave Jason tells Colette,

"This cabana is reserved for us – you, me and our friends."

They are both excited, like children, and they walk out; Colette in the direction of the girls, and Jason off in the throng of happy, impressed people. Colette walks in the direction she last saw the girls, but they are no longer there. Hmm, she gracefully moves through the room, observing Jason's tastes and enjoying getting more familiar with him in this way. They are so similar yet, obviously different.

Jason is in the crowd, asking everyone if they're okay, and if the hors d'œuvres are tasty, and if they'd like more of anything please don't hesitate to ask one of the wait staff. He wants this to be a huge success. He's hoping the Los Angeles Times reporter is enjoying herself, and that the New Yorker food columnist thinks Neylan's is the new best spot for foodies. Colette literally bumps into him and looks at his face – she can feel him. Though he appears to be composed, somehow, she knows he's nervous inside. She slips her hand inside the fold of his arm and begins walking with him around his party. She starts saying soothing things to him, helping him to come back to his center. Now the composed façade is real. Jason is back, and at that instant a reporter begins a conversation with him. Colette easily slips her arm out of his and gracefully walks away.

Walking through the crowd, Lauren and Pamela finally spot Colette.

"Now this is a party," Pamela says to Colette.

"You certainly know how to select a guy with your taste."

Colette smiles and leads them over to the cabana. As they're entering, Colette informs them that this is a reserved space for the six of them. She feels privileged and honored. Pamela and Lauren appreciate Jason's generosity. When they open the curtains to the private lounge, they see a table set up as a bar with beautiful wines, top shelf liquor, allowing them to pour whatever their pleasures. There are also trays of delicious food, deserts, and water, flat and carbonated.

"Jason really knows how to take care of his friends," Lauren says.

"This is beautiful," Colette responds.

She stands in the entry way and takes it all in. She has a clear picture of the man she loves. *The cream of the crop,* she thinks. She takes a seat. Shortly after the girls are situated, Jason, James and David walk in. They all have drinks in their hands and are animated. They have interacted with people they all need to know. It is becoming a wonderful networking opportunity. When they see the girls are there, Jason becomes a bit antsy. He looks at the guys and James does something with his cellphone, and the head waiter walks in with a tray of champagne. He extends the tray to all and each person takes a glass. The head waiter looks at Jason, who nods his head. He waiter exits the cabana. Jason then stands in front of them and raises his glass.

"I have two very important things to say," Jason begins.

Everyone is paying attention to Jason.

"First, I'd like to thank you all for your support; for being here tonight. But I'd really like to thank the other two of us," he says, while looking at James and David,

"for designing this restaurant with me, and for believing in my dream. I'd also like to thank Pamela and Lauren for supporting the relationship that Colette and I have developed; and again, for being here tonight. I know the two of you are as close to Colette, as those guys over there, are to me. That's why I hope to one day be a part of that closeness – the same way I want Colette to be that, to the two guys that mean the world to me."

Colette is looking at Jason with love-filled eyes. She's thinking he is the best man she's ever known. She loves him. With that said, Jason walks over to Colette. He stands in front of her and reaches into his pocket. David and James look at each other. Pamela and Lauren also look at each other with curiosity. Colette is so wrapped up in her own thoughts that this moment is not really registering – until Jason gets down on one knee and takes Colette's hand. She sits there quiet with a stunned look on her face.

"Colette, since the day I met you, I knew you were the one for me. *Tu es mon rêve.* You are my, woman. I have loved you since our walk, in Naples after dinner at Michael's, the day after we met."

Jason began removing something from his pocket. It was a small box. He opened it and removed a beautiful ring. The diamond was large, yet tastefully set in white and yellow gold.

"Will you marry me Colette? Will you be my wife?"

Colette could not speak. She wrapped her arms around Jason's neck. She began to cry. Colette held Jason tightly. She still couldn't find her voice, but she shook her head yes and looked in his eyes, which were tearing up.

"So, is that a yes?" Jason asked.

Finding her voice, Colette whispered,

"Yes, I'll marry you. I will be your wife, Jason English."

Jason lifted Colette off the ground and turned her around in a circle, so happy she said yes.

"She said yes!! She's going to be my wife!" he began to say to all in the room.

Pamela and Lauren were in shock and came over to hug Colette. All the girls were crying. They were looking at the ring, telling Colette how stunning it was.

James and David walked over to shake Jason's hand, and they all embraced. Then they walked over and congratulated Colette. Jason is ecstatic. He can't believe that he's going to be Colette's husband. James walks over and picks up a bottle of champagne and begins topping off everyone's glass. The party has only just begun. The four friends left Colette and Jason in the cabana. Everyone was high on the excitement of the proposal. The entire night was a lot to take in.

The two are standing near the makeshift bar in the cabana. Colette is still trying to comprehend what just happened. She's a little giddy from the champagne and her full heart. *She is engaged! Jason English has proposed to her.* As they stare into each other's eyes, Colette broke out in a huge smile that was followed by laughter.

"I love you Jason English! I can't believe I'm going to be Mrs. Jason English!" Colette expressed.

Jason took her face in his hands, and began issuing tiny kisses all over her face. When he got to the tip of her nose, he slowly went to her lips and kissed her top lip. Then he kissed her bottom lip. He then went to each corner and kissed those before he delicately covered her mouth with his and kissed her with all of the passion he could convey in a cabana – at the grand opening of Neylan's..

"I know you drove here, but I don't want to be without you tonight," Jason expressed.

He looked deeply at her. Jason wanted her – now. He could feel himself rising and he slowly pulled away.

"Would you stay with me tonight? I'll handle the girls and your car. There's no need to concern yourself with that."

Colette wanted Jason as well.

"I don't want to be anywhere else, Jason English."

She stepped closer to him and pressed her body against his. She could feel him and that excited her. Looking intensely at Jason, Colette told him she cannot wait to be alone with him. They exchanged a naughty glance and Jason took her hand and they walked out of the cabana to join the party.

The head waiter walked over to them. Jason acknowledged him and immediately escorted Colette to a platform in the center of the room. Colette didn't notice it before. The two walked up the few stairs leading them to the flat surface. Jason took the microphone, which seemed to be waiting for him. The staff were making certain everyone's glass was full of whatever they were enjoying. The music was down to a whisper and then came the sharing of his absolute good fortune. James, David, Lauren and Pamela were directly in front of the microphone. *You've got to give it to the head waiter. ...*

"Ladies and Gentlemen. The opening of Neylan's is a dream come true and I would like to take this time to raise my glass to each, and every one of you! I cannot thank you enough for your presence tonight – such support. You are the people I am excited about preparing meals for in the future," Jason proclaimed as he took a sip of his champagne.

"I have another announcement to make."

Jason glances at Colette, and says,

"Although Neylan's *est mon rêve*, Colette *est mon rêve*. I have asked her for her hand in marriage and she has accepted. This beautiful lady said yes, to sharing her life with me! Tonight is the happiest night of my life!"

Jason embraced Colette and held her tightly, kissing her deeply, yet respectfully. The guests were happy and gave them a roaring round of applause.

"Celebrate with us! The party has just begun," Jason said to all in the crowd.

As he and Colette exited the platform, someone touched the back of Jason's left arm. He turned around to see Suzette standing there. Her face was beaming with joy and a hint of sadness.

"*Félicitations mon cher Ami.»* she said.

Colette looked at the woman and felt sorry for her for a brief second. Even though the woman was beautiful and beaming, there was something sad about her that Colette noticed. Jason responded in French to Suzette's congratulations as she walked directly up to Colette.

"*Bonjour,*" Suzette greets Colette warmly.

Colette is not sure if the woman she is meeting has been crying or if she just carries that expression.

"You are going to make a beautiful bride. Congratulations."

Suzette then turned swiftly, and gracefully made her egress. Jason was getting ready to explain who Suzette is, but Colette was on a cloud and, really not interested. He took her by the hand and together they mingled happily as a newly engaged couple.

Suzette ended up at the bar requesting a Hendrick's and St.-Germain martini. She stood there alone wondering if what she'd just heard was correct. She knew it must be, she's here and she heard it with her own ears. What was she thinking? She and Jason could have never made it work. Delice continues to have a solid place in her heart and Jason found his true love the same day they'd gone for their first run together. She doesn't even live in the States. This – asking herself if something she has witnessed is true – is an old habit she's been trying to break ever since Delice took a lover and she saw them together.

Suzette doesn't fare too well with disappointment. She's never really had to be bothered with experiencing those kinds of emotions, until Delice. Her father wouldn't hear of it. Not his little girl. He knew she'd have a wonderful life; he's seen to that. But keeping her safe from heartbreak was another story all together. Standing at the bar, Suzette realized Jason was standing next to her. She looked up at him. Embarrassed. Jason looked down at her and askedher if everything was all right. He was worried. He knew she'd been going through it with Delice. He wanted her to have a good time.

"Jason, she's beautiful. I saw the love for you in her eyes. *Lui faire plaisir mon ami.*"

When Suzette said that to Jason, he knew she was thinking about her failed relationship with Delice.

"I plan on making her happy for the rest of her days. But I'm worried about you Suzette. There is a sadness in your eyes," said Jason, searching her face for answers.

Since they'd met the two of them had become pretty close.

"If you are wondering if I have seen him,"

her voice trails off as she took a polite sit of her martini,

"I have not; yet we did have a few words the day before I departed to the States."

"I take it the conversation didn't go the way you would have liked," Jason insinuated.

"You are correct. But why would I expect anything else from a man who has decided to take a lover right under my nose." Suzette barked.

She was on the verge of self-pity, when Colette slipped her arm through Jason's.

"Come with me Baby." Colette was seductive.

She was sexy, happy and ready to take Jason away with her. She thought, *how long is that woman going to be sad? She's at an exciting, celebratory event.*

"Excuse us," Colette said with a smile at Suzette as she took Jason away.

"Is she all right, Jason? She looks so sad." Colette was concerned about Suzette as well.

"I'm not sure. I went over to her because her behavior was interesting when she came and congratulated us," Jason says.

"Who is she?" Colette asked.

"She seems sad. When she came up to me after your speech she seemed a little far away. What's her story?"

"I purchased this building from her. That's how we met." Jason was opened about it.

"Oh," Colette says.

"Is she a real estate agent?"

"No. Her grandfather owned the property. He's passed away and left her to handle much of his estate. Neylan's was one of the properties," Jason tells Colette.

"I'm sorry for her loss. It's strange how that happens – something that brings someone sorrow, delivers someone else so much joy."

Colette's words were mellifluous as she looked at Jason. They both shared a quiet moment.

Jason felt proud, having an opening better than he'd imagined and asking Colette for her hand in marriage. He couldn't believe this was happening. He thought about the day he returned from Paris, and that lonely feeling that enveloped him as he surveyed his empty house. He remembered the talk he had with the guys about being ready to find *his* woman. He stole a glance of the face of his fiancé as she talked casually to their friends. Warm and content – that is how he was feeling.

The only people remaining were the six of them, the wait staff and the cleanup crew. They were all feeling tired, but also accomplished. They'd done a spectacular job! It almost felt like little elves had come to help. Colette's car had been taken to Jason's house during the opening celebration. The guys had secured a car for the occasion, so no problem getting Pamela and Lauren home. Everything seemed to have been done in a twinkle.

After saying their goodbyes, David and James accompanied Pamela and Lauren home. Jason met with the wait staff and they handled the particulars of splitting tips, reorganizing the restaurant and restocking any residual alcohol. Once Jason knew all was in order, he and Colette got into an awaiting car. Their exhaustion didn't shadow the excitement they were feeling, as a result of their new status. In the car Colette removed her shoes, placed her legs over Jason's and leaned back against the corner of the back seat. She closed her eyes. Jason put his hand on her leg and gently stroked it. He looked at Colette. He knows she can't resist his touch. Her eyes slowly opened.

"I'm here Jason English, and I feel you," She said in a soft voice.

She rearranged her legs and moved closer to him. She leaned over and kissed him.

"I want something that you've got, Mr. English."

Colette was looking directly into Jason's eyes with intense mischief. They were very near Jason's house.

"I think I have an idea Ms. Abraham. Let me find out if it's what I think it is."

Jason whispered something in her ear and Colette blushed.

"That's exactly what I want."

She placed her hand on his inner thigh and squeezed gently. The car pulled into the driveway and the driver jumped out and opened the door on Colette's side first. Jason had to handle some business with the driver so he walked Colette to his front door to let her in and quickly took are of the driver. When he got to the threshold, he stood there thinking, *That's my woman*, as he watched Colette slowly step out of her dress, and stare at him with that look. She stood there and slowly – but not like a strip tease – began to remove her jewelry, starting with her bracelet. Before she got to her earrings, Jason had her pinned passionately against the wall and was all over her.

"Is this what you were asking me for?" Jason was breathing heavily.

His desire was evident. He was handling her a bit roughly, but with care. Colette's breaths were accompanied by little high pitched moans.

"Yes." She said in a whisper,

"This is exactly what I want. I want all of you."

*t seemed as though the car had gotten to Huntington Beach really quickly. They arrived at Pamela's house first. And here's where things became confusing for everyone. James requested that the driver allow him to see Pamela in and come retrieve him once David saw Lauren home safely.

All eyebrows were raised, yet nobody said anything. Not even Pamela. The driver's eyes swept the faces of all in the car before he graciously agreed and pulled away. Standing in front of her house, Pamela looked at James with concern.

"Is everything all right. Is there something going on with Colette and Jason that I should know about?" Pamela didn't know what to think.

"No, no. It's nothing like that," James said to reassure her.

"Well what is it?" Pamela asked.

"May we go inside?" James asked.

"It is late and I'd rather you be comfortable. They'll be back to get me really soon and I'd like to talk to you."

Pamela had no idea what was going on, but she had no problem spending any time with James. She could see herself with him. Pamela never discussed her attraction to James with anyone. It had been quite some time since she even considered a relationship, but lately she'd been thinking she would like to have someone in her life.

"Certainly, we can go inside."

She smiled at him and unlocked the door. Once in she invited James to have a seat. He was surprised that he was nervous. *It took a party and liquid courage for you to tell this girl what you've been thinking since you met her the first time*, James thought. *Well, here goes.*

"Pamela, I apologize if I caused you any concerns. I know it may have been unexpected for me to have asked the driver to essentially, drop me off here." He laughed uneasily.

"I just wanted some time alone with you, even if for a brief moment."

James felt better, he got it out. Whew! Pamela was very interested in what he had to say. James became comfortable once he expressed the beginning portion of his thoughts. *Is this going where I think it is?* Pamela asked herself. *If it is, it's about time something in this arena goes in my favor.*

"Perhaps I'm making this a big production because I'm interested in you. I have been since we were first introduced," James said, wondering what she was thinking.

"Well, James that's news to me. I'm thrown off guard."

As Pamela spoke James listened intently.

"May I ask why it's taken this long to let me know how you feel?" she inquired.

"It's a lot, so I'll just say that I haven't been ready to be in a serious relationship," he replied.

"I think David will be here shortly to pick me up. I'd like to invite you to dinner on Thursday night, or whenever you have a free evening."

Pamela was smiling at the invitation.

"I think dinner will be nice. I'd like to hear all about it – why you haven't been ready to be in a serious relationship."

"Fantastic. How do you feel about dining at Geoffrey's in Malibu?" James asked.

He was feeling good now.

"That sounds fine," Pamela said.

And by the way, Thursday evening is good with me."

They sat in silence for a moment before James received a text from David informing him the car was out front. James told Pamela that David had arrived, then he asked her for her telephone number. Pamela gave it to him and he stored it in his cellphone. They both stood up and she walked him to the door to let him out. James leaned forward and kissed her goodbye on the cheek. He winked at her and she closed the door.

Pamela stood there for a brief moment. *Nice*, she thought. *What a way to end a fabulous evening*. James got into the car and smiled at David.

"So, you finally mustered up the nerve. I've seen how you look at her whenever we're around her and Lauren."

David said the words with pride. Smiling at James he added,

"You will not live to regret it, so tomorrow I don't want to hear anything from you if it's not supporting your brilliant decision."

James looked over at David with the expression of a little boy.

"I was attracted to her the first time Jason introduced us to her and Lauren. Then after the small dinner party Colette hosted for all of us back in March, something about her captured me. I just never really talked about it," James said.

"What was the reason for your silence?" David inquired.

"It was Jason's time, Dave. He had just gotten home from France, and we'd already begun to make our mark. He needed something to be his. Then he met Colette and that – the love at first sight thing – was his. I wasn't into establishing a relationship with anyone. And when I couldn't stop thinking about Pamela, I decided against discussing it to let Jason have his …" James paused.

"I just had to be certain. I didn't want to bring anyone into my personal confusion, especially if that someone was Colette's friend. Too close to home."

David sat and listened to his friend. He was astounded that Pamela would be the one to bring James back. Not that there was anything wrong with Pamela. He silently shook his head and chuckled. *Talking about a family affair.*

"I really like her, and not the way, or for the reasons I usually like someone," James explained to David.

"I'm taking her to Geoffrey's Thursday night."

"Well," David said, as he patted James on the shoulder.

"I say it's about damned time!"

They both laughed and enjoyed the early morning ride down Pacific Coast Highway.

Shrimp Benedict
(Two Bunch Palms Essence Restaurant)

Poached egg
Tiger prawn
Canadian bacon
Organic spinach
English muffin
Hollindaise

Thirteen

MANHATTAN BEACH, 2010
TELLING

It was a lazy Sunday morning in Manhattan Beach. Jason woke up to Colette, tucked safely in his arms. He reached over and kissed her sleepy forehead. She made a sweet smile and nestled closer to him. It was obvious neither one of them wanted to move. They lay quietly for a few more moments before Jason gently took Colette's left hand and looked at the ring she had accepted last night. He then returned her hand to its relaxed position, extended that same free arm and picked up the phone.

"Bonjour maman et dad. Well tout cela était une énorme ouverture de restaurant success. The et la proposition."

When Colette heard Jason speaking French, she knew he was talking to his parents. She opened her eyes and looked at him, expecting the phone to come her way. Jason wanted his mother to speak with her and she knew it. She loved his mom and was ready to squeal with delight with her! Sure enough, he handed the phone to Colette and he eased out of bed.

Jason had freshened up, did his thing in the kitchen and come back in the room with coffee, croissants, and strawberry jam, to find the two women still on the phone. By this time, Colette was sitting up in bed, wide awake. She was as bright as the sun, surrounded by the hues of the rainbow as she talked and shared with animation to his mom. Jason held out his hand and wiggled his long, strong fingers for the phone. He was smiling at Colette.

"Ok mom, your favorite baby-boy has his hands out for you."

She smiled lovingly at Jason as she said,

"I love you too, and can't wait until you guys get here."

She returned the phone to Jason and got out of bed and quickly walked out of the room. When Colette re-entered, Jason was sitting in bed and had the covers on her side pulled back for her to get in and sit next to him. On the breakfast try, her coffee was poured with cream and no sugar. Jason liked his black. She slid under the covers, picked up her cup, and blew it before she had a sip.

"Thank you, Baby," She said.

Colette kissed him lightly on the lips and looked at him with bright eyes.

"I never thought I would marry a man who could prepare 'all things food' better than I." she complimented.

"Sweetheart, consider yourself privileged. They ask a pretty penny for personal chefs, and yours comes with benefits." He raised an eyebrow then winked at her.

"Do you know how sexy you are Jason English?" Colette almost purred the question.

Jason removed the tray from the bed and said,

"Come here my fine feline."

Columbia, South Carolina, 2015

When Colette walked away from Jason, he appeared stupefied. Shaking off the feeling, he gets up and follows her. Realizing she's going into the kitchen helps him to feel a little relieved, yet perplexed. Colette sits at her favorite spot at the table and with her hand, gently pats the place Jason has come to know as, his seat. He stands over the chair for a brief moment before he sits in it. Colette begins the conversation.

"Jason. I'm really confused. I know in my gut that what's going on doesn't involve infidelity, so what's really going on."

Since sitting at the kitchen table she has composed herself as if a switch has been turned on. She is looking at him with both compassion and concern. Her mind is working like the skilled hands of a Rubik's Cube master.

"*Dieu merci!*" Jason exclaims.

He's disappointed in himself and sorry he's allowed his love for Colette to be questioned by her and that his behavior has aroused suspicion. He could kick himself for handling the Suzette thing so inappropriately.

"The other person involved is a woman. It's Suzette," Jason says.

He looked Colette straight in the eyes.

"And you're right. Nothing has ever happened between us."

"Would you like to start from the beginning?" she asks.

Colette is determined to be with Jason no matter what the problem, thinking, *We can get through this.* Jason feels appreciative that something that could have been a huge catastrophe is being handled with such care. No thanks to him. He knew exactly where to begin and that is where he started.

"I met Suzette the day before I met you. The Monday I arrived from France, I saw the sign in the window of the building that became Neylan's. I called it, got a return call from Suzette and I scheduled a meeting with her for Thursday. As fate would have it, our paths crossed at my athletic club on Wednesday. We had a casual dinner that evening. She was upset, and I thought libations, and snacks would be nice for her. I will admit, there was a glimmer of a spark between us, but I didn't want to mix business with pleasure. We met for a run the next morning and she informed me she was returning to Paris in the next couples of days. There was no time for anything to come of it and that was all right with me.

That night I attended the wine tasting at Tin Roof. When I met you, I knew you were the one for me, and any thought of her in a romantic way faded to black. Although she was not on my mind in a personal way, she was the woman I had to do business with to purchase the building. We were good though, because I told her about you at our next meeting when I signed the purchase papers. She in turn discussed Delice, her fella of many years, and her love for him and their difficulties. We started to become good friends then, and have been friends ever since."

Jason paused to come up for air, and Colette said one word.

"Paris."

"Yes. I had planned to attend the food exhibition in Paris alone because I knew I'd be busy. Hence the reason you didn't accompany me. Suzette knew of the event and put out some feelers for me. Of course, she knows all of the heavy hitters there so she arranged some promising meetings for me. I was in heaven at the exhibition and really excited about what could happen if I met the right person to partner with. You know I want to have a sweet little bistro in the *le troisième arrondissement*. Suzette owns some property there that she was considering selling or leasing to me for a song. I'd be there for the event so we scheduled a dinner on my last night in the city," Jason explains.

Jason's look is no longer one of bewilderment or fear. He knows Colette believes him. His eyes are filled with deep gratitude.

"On my last night there, Suzette and I went to dinner at one of the most, posh restaurants in Paris. It was a celebration. I was going to lease a building from Suzette in the 3rd *arrondissement*. My reason for being there worked out perfectly. I was introduced to fabulous people and I was walking away with more than I expected in terms of education, recipes and knowledge of particular foods. At dinner, Suzette's connections kept the champagne flowing and we were having a grand time. When I escorted her home, I saw her inside. She made a big pot of coffee and we were planning our – yours and mine – return visit to the city to look at the building. I thought you'd love the trip and perhaps you and Suzette could get to know each other a little better, but here is when everything shifted," Jason says.

"Suzette started coming on to me. I didn't think I had been behaving inappropriately. But maybe there were residual feelings from years past. I wasn't sure if that was the case or not. I knew we had had far too much to drink. She became more seductive – flirty, and at first I thought it was cute. We were just being how we'd been in the past – friends – when she came over to me and stood really close. I didn't take a step back, I stood there. We looked at each other.

She touched my hand and picked it up and placed it on her breast. I didn't move. I allowed it. The whole thing was surreal, like an out-of-body experience. I kept thinking, she knows I'm married to Colette. I was wondering what she was doing. Then, as if reading my mind she told me it's natural for a man to take another lover, and she kissed me. I kissed her back. And as she was attempting to kiss me again, I took a giant step backward. I told her this couldn't happen and I apologized if I gave her the wrong impression. Well, Suzette's used to getting her way. She came back to me and tried to kiss me again.

"By this time, I felt fully sober, aware of my actions and told her I wasn't interested in her that way. She then began undressing. I tried to talk to her and she began crying and saying things about the building and her connections. She didn't seem anything like the women I had come to know. She was behaving like a spoiled brat. I knew she was intoxicated and would probably feel bad in the morning. I shouldn't have returned her kiss. I'm a married man, and even though I was inebriated, I was totally out of line within the confines of our marriage. I was disgusted at myself for disrespecting you, our marriage and myself. I was ashamed of myself for my participation in any of it. When she continued her tirade, I left, securely locking and closing the door behind me." Jason poured his heart out, looking directly at Colette.

"My behavior here at home after all of this is inexcusable. I didn't tell you this before because I didn't want to jeopardize our marriage any more than I already have. I am embarrassed and I apologize, Letty," Jason finished.

Colette looked at him.

"I knew there was something about her; always sad and needing to talk to you all of the time. I don't like the fact that you kissed her, or the fact that she invited you to take her as your lover. I'm the only lover you need. I know life is full of variety and women are beautiful. You're a beautiful man – inside and out. You're also sexy. But you are my beautiful, sexy man. Women are going to come on to you, sweet darlin', but the next time, and there will be a next time, don't let it get that far."

For some strange reason, Colette is not upset. She is pretty relieved, knowing the man she believed Jason to be, is who he is. She leans over to him and whispers,

"I love you."

Jason can't help but continue to thank God for blessing him with Colette.

"You don't have to ever worry about anything like this happening in our lives again. You can bet money on it," Jason says to her.

"So, now that it's all out, what did you decide about the building and the restaurant in the *3rd arrondissement*? Are we going to open something up there?"

Colette was curious and didn't want to allow someone to have control over Jason's decisions.

"Since those shenanigans with Suzette, I've decided not to do anymore business with her. Our friendship is okay, as she was very embarrassed and sorry for her behavior. We had a long conversation about it, but there is no more solo friendship with me without you. If you can forgive her, she will be *our* friend. Not just my friend. And as far as the bistro there, it will happen, but you and I will venture over and decide. We'll do it our way," Jason says.

"Jason," Colette says, looking sleepy and drained,

"Come to bed with me. I don't want to talk anymore."

"Okay, Baby. Let me put you to bed."

Jason took her hand and they were both ready to go to sleep.

Sundried Tomato and Fetta Frittata

Organic eggs
Sundried tomatoes
Garlic
Fetta cheese
Basil
Salt
Pepper
Chili Pepper Flakes

Mix all ingredients
Place in a greased cast-iron skillet
Bake at 350 degrees

Fourteen

The Monday morning after the opening of Neylan's, the girls had decided to have breakfast together. They all took the day off and they were glad they did. They knew it was going to be a big weekend, but no one had any idea Colette would be engaged today. They had things to talk about.

Pamela decided to make brunch, complete with mimosas. Eleven o'clock on the dot and Colette stepped into the house. Left hand extended and with the attitude of grandeur. Pamela looked at her and said,

"You'd better stop it." They laughed.

"Let me see it again," Pamela said. She wanted to see the ring again up close in the light of day. Colette showed her the ring, this time she was serious and humble.

"It's beautiful. You think James might have good taste like Jason?" Pamela was trying to bring up the conversation about James.

"No, you didn't Pamela," Colette said, looking at her with mouth agape.

"No, I didn't! You know me better than that. Although he did surprise me on Saturday night."

Pamela began telling Colette about the happenings after the driver stopped in front of her house and James practically invited himself in. Colette was stunned in a good way.

"Well you finally put it out there. Your intentions have been to meet some-one. Right?" As Colette awaited her response, the front door opened, and it was Lauren. Bright eyed and buzzing. They could tell she also had a story.

"How nice of you to make us girls a homemade brunch, Pamela," said Lauren.

She was always thoughtful and complimentary.

"So, who wants to start?" she asked.

"First things, first. Who wants a mimosa?" Pamela said.

Six hands, including hers went up, followed by loud laughter. She had already prepared a tray of them. She brought it over and let each person select their own.

"Now," Lauren said,

"Who wants to begin? I can feel we all have a story this morning!"

She began to giggle with joy. They all looked at her.

"What?" Lauren questioned.

"Well," Colette began.

"I think one of you should start, since I have answers to questions I know you all have." She smiled slyly.

"Okay, I'll go."

Pamela began the story about James coming over on the escort home.

"I was going to call you yesterday to ask you about that Pamela, but I decided to wait until this morning, to spare you having to repeat the story," Lauren quips with a smile.

"You've all heard me comment on James. Sometimes I may speak to how sexy he is, or perhaps I've talked about his business savvy. No matter what I've said, if you've been paying attention, you've picked up the clue that I like him," Pamela says to them.

"Are those expressions of 'I didn't know'?" she asked.

"Kind of. You never like anyone, Pamela," Lauren commented.

"I didn't think to pay attention. But now that I know you like him, I'll have perked ears," says a playful Lauren.

"I remember you placing the intention of wanting to be in a relation-ship, and that it's slowly manifesting doesn't surprise me at all," Colette said.

"Tell us what happened once you were inside together."

Pamela reiterated the story in its brief entirety.

"So, as it stands, we're having dinner at Geoffrey's in Malibu on Thursday night. I'm really interested in his story. He'd started to tell me why he hasn't been in a relationship but then David was back to retrieve him. That's all I've got girls. We'll pick up where this is leaving off."

Pamela looked over at Lauren.

"So?"

Lauren began to laugh nervously.

"Why are you looking at me?"

She looked like the cat that ate the canary.

"Okay. I spent last weekend with Danny. We were in Beverly Hills at the Four Seasons. He always spoils me, especially when he wants something," says Lauren, with a radiant smile on her face.

The room was silent.

"Isn't anyone going to ask me what he wants?" Lauren said.

"What does he want, Lauren?" Colette asked.

"Me!" Lauren shoots back.

"He wants me. But even though I'm smiling and flattered – and you all know how much I love Danny – I'm not sure if getting back together with him makes any sense."

She looked at both Colette and Pamela. They all knew how much Lauren loves Danny, and they also knew how tumultuous the relationship has been – from the very beginning. Pamela was the first to speak.

"Now you know I'm the one who will tell you what I really think. That's what friends do."

Pamela paused and looked at both women. She continued with her concerns.

"I think reconciling with Danny would be a mistake. If you could remove the physical passion, that animal attraction, I don't believe you would consider this as an option. He's the guy who hurts you, Sweetie. You know I'm right."

"I have to agree with Pamela, Colette says.

"We love you, and we see how things are between the two of you. I know we can't tell you how to conduct your affairs, or how to live your life …"

Lauren jumps in.

"I don't mean to interrupt you Colette, but I know you are both right. I just want to milk this good feeling for a while. I want to hold on to the dream that this could really work."

Lauren began to cry.

"I keep asking myself why I put myself in this predicament. I didn't have to love him. I could have walked away," Lauren sobbed.

The girls held Lauren. Neither one said another word. Colette fetched tissues and Pamela got the Hendrick's. She looked at Colette, who nodded her head approvingly. They resolved this day was going to be one of long conversations and libations. Luckily, they had reserved the day for each other. Lauren composed herself briefly and apologized for putting a damper on the brunch. Pamela told her she was making her a dirty martini and she didn't want an argument from her. Lauren extended her hand, reaching for the drink and looking at Pamela and Colette with sad eyes. Pamela placed it in her grasp and they all moved to the comfy couch in the living room.

"How are you Lauren?" Colette inquired.

"I'm good. Just feel foolish for blubbering all over you two." Lauren tried to give it some humor. She was embarrassed.

"Don't you dare." Colette scolded.

"We are here for you no matter what. Crying is never blubbering, and we won't let you joke about this. We know you're hurting."

"I know, but I feel bad because I love him so," Lauren says.

Lauren was now calm and relaxed. She was sipping her martini, grateful she was in the company of the love of her friends.

"He's asked me to marry him," she confided in a soft, sad voice.

"The proposal was so romantic, but I know that is no reason to wed. And even though I'm aware of what my answer will be, I asked him if I could think about it."

Her voice trailed off into a space of disappointment.

"It's good you're not going to accept for Danny's sake. If you don't mind me saying, it's a great time to put Lauren first!" Pamela said in a protective manner.

She loves her friend and didn't want to see her hurting. Colette joined the conversation.

"Sweet girl ... I know you love him. He knows it too. But it's a good time to put your happiness before his, especially now. To marry someone you know is not a fit for you will only cause sorrow for you both in the days to come."

Colette touched Lauren's hand and looked at her closely.

"You're making the right decision."

They all sat without a word. Pamela looked over at Colette. The room was still, yet the buzz of excitement remained. Pamela was happy about her encounter with James on Saturday night, or shall we say early Sunday morning, and Colette was brimming over with unbearable joy about her engagement.

Lauren broke the silence.

"Thank you both for your support. I really appreciate it. But I know you Colette. I know you are the little piñata. Why don't you just expose all the goodies? I know you have tons of them for us."

Colette began to laugh, amused her friends know her so well.

"That's our girl! I'm so glad you're better. I wasn't sure of what to do next. Okay, so Sunday morning ..."

Colette began sharing her story about Jason's mom and how happy she was to be engaged to him. Lauren's mood shifted. She was no longer upset and ready to support her friend. She was listening to the story. Pamela was trying to follow the details and not wander off into her own thoughts about the possibilities of a life that may include James.

"So, Pamela, what are you thinking about James?" Colette asked.

Pamela thought for a second.

"I don't want to get my hopes up. I'll just wait and see what Thursday night brings me."

Lauren and Colette responded in unison,

"No Pamela! You deserve to be excited," Lauren said enthusiastically.

"Think about everything you'd like to happen that evening. Imagine how good it's going to be. I'm excited for you."

"I know Lauren. I just don't want to step into anyone's scribbled backstory," Pamela said. She was speaking to both of her friends. After making the statement, Pamela realized she was afraid. She hadn't been a relationship since Michael, and the way that ended really threw her.

Pamela and Michael had something that resembled smoldering embers of passion. It was hot and steamy. He just had to look at her and they would be entangled. All Pamela had to do was merely walk into the room and he'd lose himself in her. Yet, even though they had that sexual heat, there was a warm, soft and playful connection between them as well. Sometimes they'd play together like a sister and brother would. They had a really good thing going, but they were both unable to express their true feelings. Michael revealed to Pamela he wanted to date others if he decided to do so. He told her he was not seeing anyone else at the time, but letting her know just in case. Pamela knew then that the relationship was over. She didn't want a man who didn't know she was enough. She ended the relationship, but the love they both had for each other lasted for quite some time.

"It's understandable why you want to hold your breath, but this is different. We are all encircled. I don't believe James would behave in a way that would cause friction in this family. By family, I mean all of us."

Colette said this, making a little circle with her index finger. She was referring to herself and the girls, Jason and his buddies. And of course, Colette knew the backstory on Pamela, and Michael.

"You're right, Colette. But to tell you the truth, I'm scared," Pamela said.

Pamela felt relieved that she expressed her feelings to her friends, who always think she's as strong as a rock.

"You know that Michael really threw me," Pamela said.

"I know, but this is now. It's your turn. You're smart, sexy and beautiful. Plus, you're funny. What man in his right mind wouldn't be thrilled to have you? And I'm leaving Michael out of the picture," Colette quipped.

Colette then winked at Lauren, and they all laughed. The vibe was lighter and Colette checked in with Lauren, who was so distracted with the talk about Pamela and Michael that Danny was nowhere close. They had only had the one cocktail and Pamela thought it was a good time to to have food. She brought out delicious cheeses, various fresh baked pastries, including home-made cinnamon rolls and turkey beacon. Then she put a vegetable frittata in the oven. The girls were glad to eat. The feast was buffet style on the table and they began to graze.

"Would anyone like coffee, or should I make you each your favorite drink?" Pamela asked.

She busied herself, placing butter from France on the table along with exceptional jams.

"Well, since we all have things pressing – Lauren and Danny's situation, you and James, and then me – the newly engaged girl, I think we need both," Colette said.

Colette gave a sweet smile, like a little angel, and looked at the others, for their approval. They both agreed. Pamela started grounding the organic coffee beans, and Lauren filled the coffee pot with water. Colette filled the ice bucket. The frittata was ready and they each got a plate and served themselves. For a moment, it was quiet as they enjoyed the food. Piping hot cinnamon rolls dripping with French butter, frittata and turkey beacon – it was better than delicious.

"Who wants coffee?" Pamela asked.

She is a wonderful hostess. She reached for big coffee mugs.

"I do," Colette said.

Then she got up and headed to the martini shaker. She poured St. Germain and Hendrick's gin, and shook it really hard, and poured herself her favorite. She asked each of her friends if they'd like her to make their drinks, and they did. She played bartender before she sat down in front of her food and a great cup of coffee.

"How decadent!" Lauren said.

She was happy they were all together with stories and support. She sang out,

"I love my life! It's a Monday and we three are having an amazing brunch, the best coffee and kick-ass cocktails! Who is doing this today? We are!" Lauren raised her glass and the others followed suite.

"With gratitude," said Colette, finishing the toast.

*L*ate in the afternoon the girls cleaned up the kitchen. They sat around until dusk before going to their separate dwellings. Pamela closed the door behind Colette and walked into her living room when the telephone rang. It was James.

"Hello, Pamela. This is James, I hope this is a good time to talk."

"Hi James. This is a perfect time," she responded. She waited for him to continue. She remembered to listen and not talk too frequently.

"I'm calling to follow-up on the conversation we had on Saturday night, or early Sunday Morning," James chuckled.

"Are we still on for Geoffrey's this Thursday evening? I've made reservations for 6:30."

"We certainly are. I'm looking forward to it," Pamela said.

"Wonderful! I'm looking forward to it as well," James said.

"I'll be at your house to pick you up at 4. You know how traffic is going to Malibu," added James.

"I know it can get really congested. 4 is good," Pamela told him.

"Then I'll see you Thursday."

James said goodbye and Pamela sat on her sofa smiling.

Chocolate Flourless cake (La Bete Noire recipe)

1. **Cake**
   - 1 cup water
   - 3/4 cup sugar
   - 9 Tbsp. (1 stick plus 1 tablespoon) unsalted butter, diced
   - 18 oz bittersweet (not unsweetened) or semisweet chocolate, chopped
   - 6 large eggs
2. **Ganache**
   - 1 cup heavy whipping cream
   - 8 oz bittersweet (not unsweetened) or semisweet chocolate, chopped
   - Lightly sweetened whipped cream

PREPARATION

1. **For cake:**
1. Preheat oven to 350°F. Butter 10-inch-diameter springform pan. Line bottom of pan with parchment round; butter parchment. Wrap 3 layers of heavy-duty foil around outside of pan, bringing foil to top of rim. Combine 1 cup water and sugar in small saucepan. Bring to boil over medium heat, stirring until sugar dissolves. Simmer 5 minutes. Remove from heat.
2. Melt butter in large saucepan over low heat. Add chocolate and whisk until smooth. Whisk sugar syrup into chocolate; cool slightly. Add eggs to chocolate mixture and whisk until well blended. Pour batter into prepared pan. Place cake pan in large roasting pan. Add enough hot water to roasting pan to come halfway up sides of cake pan.

3. Bake cake until center no longer moves when pan is gently shaken, about 50 minutes. Remove from water bath; transfer to rack. Cool completely in pan.

2. **For ganache:**

1. Bring whipping cream to simmer in small saucepan over medium heat. Remove from heat. Add chocolate and whisk until smooth. Pour over top of cake still in pan. Gently shake pan to distribute ganache evenly over top of cake. Refrigerate cake in pan until ganache is set, about 2 hours. DO AHEAD: *Can be made 2 days ahead. Cover and keep refrigerated.*

2. Run knife around pan sides to loosen cake; release sides. Cut cake into wedges and serve with whipped cream.

Fifteen

MANHATTAN BEACH, JANUARY, 2017
A CELEBRATION AT NEYLAN'S

Jason and Colette's fifth wedding anniversary – Janis is now engaged to Ian and her second play is coming to the Pasadena Playhouse. Karen and David are married and expecting their first child. Pamela and James are married, and Lauren is dating someone new.

Jason and Colette have decided to celebrate their fifth wedding anniversary in the South Bay since there is where they met. When they were considering places to celebrate, they agreed on Neylan's. That will be the perfect place. The conversation was leading toward a quaint dinner celebration with their closest friends at Tin Roof, until the chime of the telephone interrupted their flow. Jason's reach is longer than Colette's, so he picked up the receiver. He walked out of the room and sat on the living room sofa and began to talk. Colette continued to jot down thoughts about the dinner. Flower arrangement ideas, the menu … They have become quite the duo.

When Jason ended the call, he walked back into the office and looked at Colette.

"What have you come up with so far?" he asked.

"Just the floral arrangement ideas, and I was just beginning the menu we'd like them to prepare. Something tasty, yet light. You have any ideas you'd like to add?" Colette asked Jason.

"Well … what do you think about making our quaint dinner celebration a big soiree?" Jason was smiling now. He couldn't contain himself.

"Who was that on the phone?" Colette asked.

She was really curious, and she had no idea what Jason was getting at.

"Janis has been pretty quiet lately, don't you think?"

Jason posed the question as if trying to solve an Agatha Christie mystery.

"Yes. I wouldn't say she's been quiet, I'd say she's been up to her ears in work. Remember, she's been working on a second play," Colette said.

She was looking at Jason a-matter-of-factly. Then, the lights came on.

"Janis finished the play, didn't she?" Colette asked with excitement.

"Bigger than that, *Bébé*. She's been shopping it around and has gotten several offers. She's decided to go with the Pasadena Playhouse theater, and it opens around the time of our anniversary dinner. I didn't mention anything to her, but give me your thoughts," Jason said.

He was looking at Colette with anticipation.

"Let's do it! That girl never said one word to me that she was finished and shopping it around," Colette said.

Colette was so happy Janis was finished with the play and on her way to the big leagues.

"But I think we should make this a surprise celebration for her, just the way we surprised her for her birthday. She'll think she's coming to our anniversary dinner but we'll be celebrating both occasions. What do you think?" Colette said.

Jason was on board. This is what he loves – to celebrate – to cook – to share. Only he won't be cooking for this event.

"Okay, *Bébé*. Why not surprise David and Karen as well by including them in the celebration? They *are* expecting their first child." Jason suggests.

He's really fired up and Colette loves to see him like this.

"I think that's a wonderful idea. Who are we going to have as the chef for that evening?" Colette wants to make certain Jason isn't planning on working that night by preparing any portion of the meal. She gave him the side-eye.

"I'm steps ahead of you my darlin'. I've asked Philippe to step in and he's agreed. He'll be here two weeks before the event. You know he's got to get everything fresh and get in touch with his contacts to make sure everything runs smoothly."

As soon as Jason finished his sentence he looked at Colette. He could feel the cloud looming over her. Philippe lives in Paris and is good friends with Suzette. He'll probably inform her, as Jason hasn't revealed what happened between them to him.

"Look *Bébé*, if Suzette shows up at our affair …"

Colette interrupts him.

"If she shows up – and I have a suspicion she will – I'll handle it. It's time I dealt with her and her disrespect." Colette said.

She had a calm expression on her face, the one that means she means business. Jason knows that expression now, all too well. He looked at her and was a bit tickled because he also knows how sweet Colette is and he can't imagine her being mean to anyone. But then again, he has no idea what she may say or do. He never really knows. But pushing that aside for a moment, Jason thinks… *let us not forget our original reason for going to California at this time – it was five years ago that Colette Abraham and I said I do. This is going to be a hell of an extravaganza.*

James fastened the clasp on Pamela's necklace. They are facing the ocean view outside their bedroom window. James has built a spec house on the Strand to sale, but since he got together with Pamela, and his office is in Manhattan Beach, he's decided to keep the house and now it is their home.

"You look beautiful," James told Pamela.

"Three years have just flown by. Are you still the happiest woman on the planet?"

James was flirting and wanting her to stroke his ego. He's been working on his need for reassurance.

"Of course I am! You bring out the best in me." Pamela smiled at James.

He offered her a shy expression, and smiled back.

"I'm glad about that, Sweetheart. I can't imagine life without you," James said.

They've been married for three years now – and they tell themselves daily that they couldn't have chosen a better partner. James finally worked through his fear of commitment. It had only taken one time for him to feel the slightest discomfort from the pain of love lost, before he opted out. He had memorized what he'd read in the book, *The Prophet* by Kahlil Gibran:

For even as love crowns you so shall he crucify you.

Even as he is for your growth so is he for your pruning.

Even as he ascends to your height and caresses your tenderest branches that quiver in the sun,

So shall he descend to your roots and shake them in their clinging to the earth.

James held on to those words until he laid eyes on Pamela. He just couldn't shake the thought of her. Knowing Pamela gave him the desire to settle down. She was understanding and kind. He had been the only one of the guys to be flying solo longer than he'd really wanted to be. First Jason met his girl. Actually, he'd met two great women in the course of one week! David had Karen. James kept wondering why he was the only one that couldn't find his *somebody*. He kept noticing Pamela. Her kindness, her sense of humor and, she was so cute. …

Pamela also faced her fear of being hurt again, when she finally admitted to her friends that day in December at brunch, that she was afraid to get involved with anyone, or to expect anything other than what she had experienced with Michael. She really didn't want to replay that portion of her life. She'd thought that he was the one. Since she mustered up the courage to allow James into her life, things took a positive turn. Thank God, she admitted her fears to her friends; that was her turning point. They all gave her sound suggestions.

"I can't imagine life without you either." Pamela said.

She walked over and stroked James' back.

"Are you ready for the car Sweetheart?" James asked Pamela before he picked up the phone.

＿＿＿

Karen and David are already in Los Angeles. They've had to keep two residents since David has become a principle actor – to his surprise. The decision was made, and at a good time too, as it wouldn't be good for Karen to fly so frequently now that she's pregnant. With all that's been going on in their lives, the new career shift for David, the move to L.A., and now the news of a new member of the family, their lives have changed tremendously. Karen really misses Colette, she is so excited to see her tonight.

David can't seem to keep his hands off of Karen's baby bump. Every time he's near her he finds his hands softly rubbing her belly. Karen likes it. She thinks it's sweet. She doesn't even mind the occasional photos she finds herself in since the news about her pregnancy has gotten out. David continues to live his life as usual. He doesn't have the huge status many principle actors have. He feels no need to conceal the wonderful news of a new baby.

Karen looks at her beautiful canary-yellow diamond and remembers the day she saw it in Carol Saunders jewelry store in Columbia. She looks at herself one more time. David takes her hand and they go out to the awaiting car

＿＿＿

*L*auren is getting ready for the celebration. She's wondering if she should wear her brown hair up or curl it and wear it down. She wants to look great when she reunites with the girls. It's been far too long since they've all been together. It's amazing that Pamela and James are married. *Who saw that coming?* David married Karen and now they're expecting a baby. She's missed the girls terribly and can't wait to tell them about her life. She feels she has finally put herself first, and has seen Danny for who he is. Even though he has many alluring qualities, he also knew her weaknesses. However, since their days together she's spent a lot of time doing the work, and now whatever he knows about her has no effect on her.

Lauren goes into her bedroom and pulls out her new Donna Karan outfit. Once she's dressed, she slips on her shoes and the doorbell rings. Like clockwork, Glenn is always on time – he never makes her wait. Lauren smiles when she hears the bell. The relationship is fresh and it feels good to go out with someone else. This time she has new tools and a new perspective. She isn't walking on eggshells, nor is she constantly second-guessing herself or seeking approval. Lauren feels good in her skin. Her newfound confidence is now the gift inside such a beautifully wrapped package.

Lauren opens her front door. …

*C*olette closes the lid of her suitcase and makes sure Jason hasn't forgotten anything in his. She zips up both garment bags and checks the time again. She looks at the airline tickets and walks over to Jason and hands them to him.

Accepting the tickets and placing them in his man bag, Jason looks at Colette and then he looks off as if in thought.

"You know," he begins,

"if I was the one to say where my life would be right now, I wouldn't have said it'd be here.

... Married to a wonderful woman, still with my best friends, and the owner of two successful restaurants. Man, Baby, I'd say life has been pretty good to me."

Colette agrees.

"I wouldn't have placed me here – in this life – with you. It's been amazing." Colette said.

She also wanders off in thought. They snap out of their brief reverie when Colette suggests they head out. They both secure their bags, and roll them out to the car. They head to West Columbia to the airport.

⌒

The Gulfstream G650 lands on the tarmac in Santa Monica. The door opens and Suzette breathes in the California sunshine, and blesses her new place of residence.

"*Il est si bon d'être de retour,*" she says as she dons her Prada sunglasses to protect her deep brown eyes.

The End

⌒

www.ingramcontent.com/pod-product-compliance
Lightning Source LLC
Chambersburg PA
CBHW051837020726
47502CB00005B/1828